Donald Readerlear born 21/02/1947 in Carshalton, UK, left Christmas 1965 to live in New Zealand, met Dennis Galvin in July 1968 and had a civil union for 48 years. Dennis Galvin passed away in September 2016. Since then, he has written an unpublished work and his published book, *The Wind That Blows*, and four more to come, all are murder mysteries. He now lives with his constant companion, Stella, a black standard poodle. He works as a caregiver part time and is a teacher of Scottish country dancing. He has devised nine published dance books, has a lovely home and a tropical garden.

This book is dedicated to Dennis Galvin, my civil union partner of 48 years; missed and always loved.

Donald Readerlear

The Wind That Blows

Austin Macauley Publishers
LONDON · CAMBRIDGE · NEW YORK · SHARJAH

Copyright © Donald Readerlear (2020)

The right of Donald Readerlear to be identified as author of this work has been asserted by the author in accordance with section 77 and 78 of the Copyright, Designs and Patents Act 1988.

All rights reserved. No part of this publication may be reproduced, stored in a retrieval system, or transmitted in any form or by any means, electronic, mechanical, photocopying, recording, or otherwise, without the prior permission of the publishers.

Any person who commits any unauthorised act in relation to this publication may be liable to criminal prosecution and civil claims for damages.

Austin Macauley is committed to publishing works of quality and integrity. In this spirit, we are proud to offer this book to our readers; however, the story, the experiences, and the words are the author's alone.

A CIP catalogue record for this title is available from the British Library.

ISBN 9781528990301 (Paperback)
ISBN 9781528990318 (ePub e-book)

www.austinmacauley.com

First Published (2020)
Austin Macauley Publishers Ltd
25 Canada Square
Canary Wharf
London
E14 5LQ

My writing is thanks to my dear departed friend, Avril Flower, the book club. Rod, Marion, Shelley and Claire, thank you for all your support. Also, to my dear friends, Kate and Leni. My thanks to the team of Austin Macauley for all their help. I wish to acknowledge Mrs Josei Lear for all her help since my partner passed away.

Synopsis

Parul Das is an Indian woman doctor that has had a failed affair in England. She is going back to India hoping to find herself.

In doing so, she finds love, a family and a new land. Dennis Galvin, an Anglo-Indian, happily married to Susan, living in Swindon England with twins, Don and Michael. Then his happy life is thrown upside down; his wife leaves him for another man. He takes a ship back to India and meets the love of his life, Parul.

Dennis takes his twins to see his mother and father in Goa. Then he and his twins visits Parul at the tea plantation just outside Darjeeling where he meets Sutra, Parul's aunty.

The twins, Don and Michael, are taught cooking by Sutra.

Parul announces she is emigrating to New Zealand. Sutra, Dennis and the twins go too.

They board the cruise ship Electra in Calcutta bound for Australia and New Zealand. Whilst on board the Electra, there are two murders which the three detectives, Parul, Sutra and Dennis try to solve.

The twins, Don and Michael, meet three young girls on board; Tilly, Bella and Badger. Bella gets jealous and pushes Don into the swimming pool. After he is rescued, he reveals the murderers.

Once the murderers are caught, everyone looks forward to their new lives in a new land. But hate and murder still lurks there.

Chapter 1

The great vessel smashed through the waves, sending flying fish scattering in all directions.

She ploughed through, dipping and cresting, spray sent high in the air falling on her decks. This great ship, proud and queenly, rode through the sea.

Parul brought her hand to wipe the sea droplets from her face and hair. She ran her fingers through her lustrous black hair and moved them away from her eyes.

She looked across the horizon expecting to see her homeland. She so needed to be enveloped in the aroma and fragrances of spices of her beloved land.

Her heart was sore and broken. She needed to add focus to her life. Her land, she knew, would renew her whole being. A stray tear ran down her cheek mixing with the sea spray.

It seemed too long ago; she still could recall the smell and perfume waft in her mind.

She loved living in Britain even after her relationship had broken up. She hated the cold winter, hated the snow and could never get used to the rain. Then came summer, but never sun and heat like India.

So, here she was, on the Atlantis, steaming to India. She would go to the Brahmaputra, hopefully to find something, but what?

First of all, she had to go to the plantation. As both her parents had died in a car accident, she had been brought up by her aunty, Sutra.

"I must go back. I need to see her again, feel her sweet arms around me to protect and love me."

She was no beauty; she had a strong jaw that was chiselled slightly; almost masculine with deep brown eyes, shoulder length hair, medium height and long slim fingers,

She felt her land and people drawing her ever nearer.

Dennis Galvin was an Anglo-Indian. Mary, his mother, was from Goa and his father, Michael, was from Yorkshire, England. He was going back to Goa. He had been married to Sally, lived very happily in Swindon in a council flat with his twin sons, Donald and Michael and their very old dog, Stella. They had been in love since they met.

One afternoon, after just coming back from work, he saw a note on the table.

He picked it up; it read: "Dennis, please forgive me, but I've felt for a year that something was missing from our marriage. Couldn't understand why I felt so sad inside. Then I met Ben. We clicked straight away. He asked me if I'd go to Australia with him. I took the boys over to Mum. When you get this note, we will be on board the Australis, sailing this afternoon for Sydney. GOD FORGIVE ME."

The last part of the note was in capitals: *Why? Why?* he thought. Somehow, *'God forgive me'* in capital letters, it infuriated him more than the rest of the note. He had not seen this coming, he thought they were happy.

"I worked shift work for the post office and many times, I came home late, but I provided a good standard of living for her and looked after her; now this!" He felt his whole life coming to an end.

What had Sally said to the boys? She's their mother? How can she leave them? What sort of creature could do that to her own children why? It was bad enough to leave me, but her flesh and blood? He remembered them being born. How proud he was of her going through all that and it was not an easy birth either.

This was the last straw. Dennis sank to his knees and wept; just for himself.

Later, he went to Jenny, his mother in law. He knocked on the door. She came out and noticed her eyes were red as she folded him into her arms.

"Don't ask me why she could do this to us, to the boys! Well, Dennis, she's no daughter of mine, I hate what she's done!"

With that, Don came out first before Michael. They both clutched on to their dad's trousers and Jenny's dress.

"Where's Mummy?" they both cried.

Dennis looked at Jenny and mouthed, "What do I tell them?"

"The truth, Dennis, they need to know right now."

She sank to her knees, "Come here, my sweet pies. Your daddy and I will look after you."

So, as best as he could, he explained to them what had happened.

A year or two passed and he felt the pain easing. One day, Dennis told Jenny he had to go back to Goa with the boys. She cried but knew that this was for the best.

"Come back, my darling. Bring my boys back."

This all rang in his ears, as all three walked up the gang plank into the vessel to take them to India.

A time to heal in his beloved country.

Chapter 2

One evening, Dennis and the boys were eating their dinner in one of the Atlantis's dining rooms. They had a full view of the rolling sea. Birds flew over the water seemingly touching the tips of the waves. They were not all that far from Port Aden.

She sat opposite the table set for eight. The other diners were a married couple from Doncaster who were sailing further than India, to Melbourne to see their grandchildren. And two Indian ladies,

Everyone made casual talk about their reasons for being on the ship. Dennis found Parul quite an interesting lady. She felt they had similar lives and both were running away and not facing their demons.

Over the days, they struck up a friendship. Both had a lot in common and both needed so much to talk about it. Both had been in love. Both had been hurt and betrayed and wanted so much to rebuild their lives but did not know how. They were naturally drawn together. Sort of kindred spirits who genuinely liked each other.

They took walks around the deck, played all sorts of deck games and became happy laughing again. The boys were being boys. Parul ran after the twins, playing hide and seek, they made her laugh; she loved children.

Time passed and they eventually docked at Bombay. At this stage, they both felt they needed each other's support though neither expressed the fact.

Dennis said, "Why don't I come to see you, after we have seen my parents? The boys have never seen a tea plantation and it would be nice for them to find out more about more what's going on."

She hugged the boys and kissed them on their cheeks. She had really become very fond of them. She, too, was looking forward to showing them around the tea plantation and she knew Sutra, her aunty, would be in her element as she just loved children too.

Then she turned to Dennis; they hugged; he held her so close neither wanting nor wishing to let go. She waved and felt a pang deep inside. She'd been happy with these three. *He's a nice man and any woman would be proud of those naughty, yet lovable, boys.*

"Dad."

"Yes, Michael?"

"Are you going to marry Parul?"

All Don could do was giggle.

"What gives you that idea?" Dennis asked Michael.

Suddenly, Don chirped, "I like her; she would make a good mummy. Our real mum has gone away. She doesn't love us, but, Parul is such fun. Don't you think so?"

Dennis put his arm around each boy, and liked what he was hearing.

He stood still for just a moment and his thoughts went back to Parul. *She loves my boys; she'd make a good mother for them.* He realised he needed to get through customs as soon as he could, as he needed to get into the hotel just for the night. Come the morning, all three needed to catch the train to Goa.

Parul watched them going she waved and blew kisses. When he looked back at her, she caught her breath. Why, she wasn't sure but she knew she hoped she would meet them again, as she waved even harder.

The days went quite quickly. She spent much time watching the waves crashing in front of the great ship as it sliced through the sea dolphin's jumping in the air playing in and out of the waves.

Looking to the horizon thinking of home.

She spent the rest of the trip, mixing with the other passengers.

Time went by quickly, and they soon arrived in the port of Calcutta with its spices wafting around her. She quickly got off the ship through customs and then straight to the station to board a train. Soon, she would arrive at the plantation and met her aunt, Sutra.

In her sixties, Sutra sat on her porch knitting, watching the birds fluttering around, just after a downpour of the first part of the usual monsoon.

She could see a small figure on the road to her home. *Was it? No, can't be;* her heart pounded in her chest. She stood up arms outstretched

"Parul?"

She shouted as tears of love ran down her cheek dripping on to her brown and yellow sari.

"Parul? Parul?"

The figure started to run, falling over her steps, her finger's reaching for the heavens.

"Sutra."

As a streak of lightning flashed across the soft rolling hills, it was followed by a tremendous role of thunder.

Both women, by now, almost touching both panting and both very wet; but, neither were caring as they met stood still then embraced each other.

"My darling, you've grown."

"Come on, sweetheart, out of the rain."

They held hands, ran for the safety of the house and changed into warm and dry clothes. While they sat sipping aromatic tea, Parul told Sutra of her life in England. Sutra responded by making a few grunts and shaking her head too.

After a long pause and looking out at the rain, which by now was very heavy, "Um, well, what now, Parul?"

"For the first time in my life, I don't know. I really don't know. I feel I'm on the point of making some sort of decision. I'm at a sign post in my life this moment is very important, Sutra."

"Yes, my dear, I think you are right."

Both looked in to each other's eyes, both hoping one or the other would suddenly say, 'Oh, yes that's what you must do'. But then just the rolling of the thunder in the distance and a knowing smile stretched across Sutra's face and she nodded.

"You'll make the right decision, my girl," she said as she lifted her hand to Parul's face and brushed a stray lock of hair from her eyes.

The days turned to weeks and Parul helped around the house, made a couple of curries, always vegetarian curries as Sutra was a Hindu. She had spent so much time in England and had got used to eating meat and English food. This was a great opportunity to taste some of Sutra's great cooking.

Most times, after eating she had gone for a walk around the plantation looking at this and that while remembering her loving parents. Then getting near to Sutra's home and the wondrous spices wafting through the air: cardamom, ginger, coriander and chilli; more and more spices hit her. She felt hungry and knew she was home at last.

The day had come to meet Dennis again. He was staying in Darjeeling in a house of a friend of Sutra. These feelings? longing! And belonging.

There he stood on the veranda holding Michael's hand both looking out and up to the sky watching birds swooping here and there.

Don came out of a side room and saw her first, "She's here! she's here!"

Dennis and Michael turned around.

The boys made a beeline for her. Parul got on her knees and scooped both up in to her arms and how wonderful she felt as she squeezed them closer. As she kissed them, a stray tear ran down her check; how she loved these boys.

And there he was with a smile that could light up a room.

"Hello, I see they are trying to smother you and I think you like it!"

"Hello, Dennis."

Parul tilted her head to one side as if to say I'll see you later; she tried so hard to walk over to him but the boys had both her hands and were busily showing her around the house. They were pulling her around the house. Both boys jabbered like starlings.

"Let me know if you need a hand."

Dennis was now bent over laughing out loud.

"See you later after those two have driven you mad."

So many questions all said at the same time. Don and Michael were trying hard to get her exclusive attention, but neither winning.

"I love you."

Don said with great emotion.

"And I do too but much and more than Don."

At this moment, she thought they were coming to blows over her.

The boys looked cross at each other. Willing to fight for their lady, like two knights in shiny armour.

"And I love you too. I love you both the same; come on you two make up."

"You first."

Michael spat out.

"No, both of you come here. Do you think a lady can choose between two fine gentlemen like you?"

With this, she eyed them knowingly and opened her arms. The boys rushed into them; all was forgotten; well, maybe for now.

Out on the veranda, she stood next to Dennis.

"So, are both your arms very long and your ear drums hurting?"

"They are boys and boys are men; only smaller thank goodness, Dennis!"

"I missed you."

Both said at the same time. He kissed her hand.

"I missed you and so did the boys, talking all the time about you on the train up here. They were driving me mad. Now, it's your turn."

He gave a very low bow and then winked, "You three! Oh my. Yes, and if you were asking, yes, I missed the two boys and their handler."

At this, she gave him a low curtsy, both burst out laughing.

The next day, they all set off for the tea plantation.

She showed them around the plantation. Sutra pranced about with the boys and playing hide and seek until she fell down on the grass, with two red Indians circling around her. She was in her element, loving every moment.

"Help me, Dennis."

"I see they've succeeded where others have failed."

Dennis and Parul laughed.

"Help! I've been captured. Well, you two, don't stand there laughing help me up, I need to start dinner."

"I'll do that, Sutra."

"I'll do it. I'm not just a pretty face, you two ladies!"

"What are you worrying about, Parul? Let him be; he knows what he's doing. Well, I hope he does."

By this time, Sutra was standing next to Parul after removing herself from the boys and a fate worse than death.

She jabbed Parul in the ribs.

"He's a nice man. You could do a lot worse."

"Stop it. No. No."

Then she realised, *Oh, how my life has changed,* but the thought quickly went.

The boys were playing. No fighting outside. Sutra had enough.

"Come inside."

After a long time, she walked to the door. They were still playing or fighting, but not listening. She lent on the side of the door frame, pointing one finger at Michael, then curling it up and back at him.

"Yes, you. Oh, and you come here too." She said in a far harsher voice.

The boys looked up, due to the tone of her stern voice caught their attention.

"Us?"

This time, Sutra said nothing but pointed inside. Face blanched, Michaels head went down; they both knew she meant business.

When they got into the kitchen, Sutra said in her sweetest voice, "Would you two help me, I need your expertise."

Accompanied by her sweetest smile, the boys wondered what was coming next.

"I think, it's time you two learnt to cook when you grow to be men and have wives?"

At this statement, both giggled.

"Take a seat, gentlemen!"

They sat facing the kitchen table arrayed with all sorts of spices and vegetables.

At this moment, Dennis and Parul came through the door. On seeing what was going on, they very quickly turned around and made a beeline outside.

"Those poor boys, Dennis."

Both could not stop laughing, Dennis got hiccups which only made Parul laugh harder. Both walked off in tears.

Each spice was laid out on the table with its name on a small bit of paper next to it. So were the vegetables.

"Now, we are going to make savoury chickpeas."

This time, the twins were silent, somewhat puzzled but interested they pointed to different things and asked quite sensible questions.

"Don. In the fridge, there's a bowl with one cup of chick peas and three cups of water. They have been in the fridge overnight. Bring it out and drain them. Michael, you are going to be my vegetable cutter man. I want you to cut up one small green chilli and take the seeds out. Now, please don't touch your eyes as it will sting them. Chop up two onions. Put them all in separate bowls. Which one of you can tell me how you peel a tomato."

"Me. Me. Me."

"Yes, Don."

"Peel it with the peeler."

"No, Don."

Both looked puzzled.

"No, Sutra. We don't know," they exclaimed.

"Put them in a bowl, cover with boiling water. Now look what happens. They are peeling themselves."

"Wow, Micky." Don said.

"Magic! You are learning lots, you two."

Now, she beamed from ear to ear. How she loved teaching these dears taking in everything. She patted both their heads and gave them a big hug.

"Michael! Into the bowl containing onions, grate two cloves of garlic, two teaspoons of ginger and ½ a teaspoon of turmeric."

"When is my job?" Don asked.

"Yours is now. We put this large saucepan on the stove to heat. Now, Don, weigh me out 30 grams of gee. This goes in the saucepan. We wait till its melted and hot. Now, I want the bowl with the onions and spices. They all go in. Now, you stir it until they look a bit soft. OK, in with the turmeric and one teaspoon of garam masala. Stir, add the water from the chickpeas, tomatoes, chilli, two bay leaves and the chickpeas. Now simmer. You see where this dial is? Turn it to simmer."

She pointed to the pan as it started to roll over with very small bubbles.

"That's it, Don hand me the lid now. This goes on top and we leave it for an hour or until the chick peas are tender and stir them from time to time."

Both boys watched transfixed while the bubbling pot like two witches waiting for their concoctions to be ready.

"Now, lift the lid. Don, squeeze me half a lemon which we can add; no pips please. Michael, chop me two tablespoons of coriander. Over there, on the windowsill, just cut some off; that's it. Now chop it up and in it goes. We are done. Your very first lesson in cooking. Well, what do you think? Off you go. Bring your dad and Parul for lunch."

Not waiting to answer both galloped out. Soon both returned pulling their captives behind them

"We cooked lunch. Really. Really."

All sat down to eat with two birds chattering all the time about what they did and how they did it, with a very wise woman looking at them. She felt *I've got to get Dennis and Parul together, I want us to be one happy family.* She thought. *I'm going to do it. Yes, I'm sure.*

Chapter 3

She lay on the bed, moonlight streaming through the shutters, the shadows like angels' wings fluttering on the walls.

What had happened? *Why?* She cast her mind back to the early morning.

She got up at her usual time. The boys had been up for some time. She heard her aunt in the kitchen making breakfast; Dennis was on the veranda sipping his favourite tea. She wandered out to him, smiling.

"Good morning, Dennis." And before he could answer, "Did you have a good sleep?"

He turned around giving her the most brilliant smile.

He looked at her. He smiled at her radiance and his fingertips just touched hers. She suddenly felt giddy and strange. The pulse seemed to radiate through her body, not stopping at bones or muscles, but wriggling down inside her then to her head. She couldn't breathe. She felt a throbbing in her throat. She, hating it, yet loved it not ever wanting it to stop.

What happened to me this morning? Tears ran down her cheeks. Then slumber came and she closed her eyes.

The dawn came, sunlight streamed through the shutters. She sat up and gazed at the room; in her mind, tiny serpents coiled and recoiled. Once again, she heard her aunt in the kitchen. She quickly banished the stray thoughts in her mind.

Today is the day for change. She got up with vigour.

"I'm going to New Zealand," Parul declared at the breakfast table.

"We don't have family in that part of the world, Parul."

"What do you mean, Sutra?"

"It'll take me some time to pack."

"You?"

"Yes, me. I may be in my sixties, but if you think I'm leaving you in a strange country, you are quite wrong."

Sutra was getting a little cross.

Parul realised she had upset her aunty.

Sutra said this with a withering look as if she was about to change Parul to a toad. Parul could only think of one of the three witches in Macbeth. Sutra gave her that radiant smile whilst shaking her head from side to side.

"If you think I'm leaving you both way across the other side of the world," Dennis remarked, "It's not happening."

"That's right, why don't we make a party of the whole thing?"

"Parul. Parul. I'm coming too and that's that."

"Well, I give in."

The following morning, Parul and Dennis organised the emigration passes and boat trip; the twins were very excited also.

So, here they all were: Parul, Sutra, Dennis and the boys, standing on the deck of this wondrous ship, 'Electra', watching their homeland go slowly out of sight. All turning to their new life. One woman not sure of herself, one older lady determined never to lose sight of the dearest girl in her heart, a man that's following his future and the woman he loves not knowing if she would return his love. Just to be near her would do, so long as his boys were happy. Don was running after Michael playing with the other children on the boat. All they could think of was the adventure in a new country.

Their adventure was about to start. New things, new ways of living and a new start to life for all.

Mrs Ethel Handeisides was sat at her dressing table combing her hair.

"Honey, sweetie, where's ma jewels?" she asked Benny.

"You'll lose ya head one day." he said in his usual effeminate voice.

Mrs Ethel Handeiside was on to her third husband, Benny Handeiside. After husband number one had been lost at sea he had left her a small oil field in Texas. Then, number two, who simply was in his eighties and dropped dead, left her a large inheritance. His two children, Martha and Steven, were not included in his will.

Ethel had never seen these two children. They didn't even attend the funeral. She couldn't care less. Besides, with this new husband, Benny was tall, very handsome and extremely effeminate. She was happy with a young gay husband and lots and lots of money.

They were on their way around the world stopping at England and then Paris. She was buying lots and lots of clothes, shoes, rings, furs, and so on.

Mr Mac Clures and his wife, Helen, came from Dundee Scotland. He was a vet and proud of it. They had travelled down to Southampton to join the ship. They were going to see their one and only son, Harold, in Brisbane Australia, where he and his wife, Brenda, had just had their first son, Adam.

They were looking forward to seeing their new grand son and his Australian wife, Brenda.

Helen had been sea sick most of the cruise and today, she felt she needed to get out and in to the sea air and feel the wind on her face.

"Are ya goan outside, ma duck?" said Cameron in his rather gruff way but kindly.

"Yes, Cameron, I thought I'd try the air. I can't stay cooped up in this cabin any longer; its driving me mad."

"Go on then. I'll bring ya a cup of broth up when you've settled ya self-down duck."

"Cameron, oh no! No! Can't stand the thought of food yet. Just let me sit in the shade near the back of the boat. After India and all those heady spices and that horrible curry. Do you know I was so ill from then on; mind you, as soon as we started going through the channel, I felt queasy, but that's sweet all the same."

She patted his hand and then left for the sea breezes which she hoped would at least clear her head.

David Pickle was on the deck, shading his eyes and fair skin from the elements watching the flying fish while congratulating himself on his bravery. At last, he was free from his nagging mother, Edwina Pickle. She had got herself pregnant at an early age and married quickly. Some years later, her husband ran away with David's school teacher; Edwina had to raise the child herself. She made sure her son wanted nothing. He couldn't do a thing without his mother demanding to know.

Here he was on his way to a new life in New Zealand; a place where he would eventually live. In this new country, he didn't know nor care; he was free for the first time in his life. *What will I do? I'd like to meet a nice girl get married.* He had seen a very pretty girl on board. He so wanted to speak to her; but oh, so shy was he. Every time she looked his way, he could feel his face going red. *I'll pluck up enough courage tonight,* he thought. *She's sat on my table for dinner tonight. Tonight's the night, yes! Yes!* He thought but the last yeses were said out loud and the American woman looked his way.

"Are ya OK, honey? Ya startled me, I nearly dropped a stitch."

She was in the middle of knitting a jersey for Benny; she really thought of Benny as her son. She had never thought of children and when she met Benny at a ball, she liked him as a son no more.

She sat on a deck chair looking out at the waves cresting then dipping, Dolly thought about her mother Lady Gwendaline Perrin. She loved her; oh, yes; but liked her? No. She embarrassed her in spite of putting on such airs and graces. After all, she had been Lord Perrin's house keeper. Jerry had married her after his first wife died in child birth and there was Gwen. She cared for him and most of all, she had Dolly, her child from her first husband, Burt, who had worked with her in a grand house in Harrogate. He passed away suddenly.

So, here she was, widowed again; but, with a title this time; how she loved the whole thing of being a lady, but sometimes when caught off guard, she would fall in to her Yorkshire slang.

"Dolly."

"Yes, Mum."

"My dear, please. Please, when we are outside of the cabin, I'm your mother."

"Mum; oh, Mother, is that better? Why do you have to put on that posh talk?"

"Let me stop you right there. Manners are everything, my dear. I do wish you would at least cultivate a much more agreeable—"

"Oh, dear, Mother."

"And don't interrupt me. You don't wait for me to finish."

This time, Dolly was a bit cross with her mother.

"Yes. Yes." she said this time in a rather cross way as Dolly was truly fed up with this constant argument.

"There. You've done it again. You're so lucky I love you."

Gwen stroked her daughter's blond hair, "I've seen you looking at that young man. He's not the right sort, my dear; we need to aim much higher than that."

"He's very handsome, don't you think mum?"

"True, but he hasn't got class, my dear."

Dolly realised this disagreement would go on and on, but he was so good looking, that, she day dreamed of setting up a home in Auckland, New Zealand. Her in the kitchen and him with his arms around her waist. Then the day dream shattered by her mother nagging her again.

Miss Stamp sat in her cabin going over the reasons why she had done something so much out of character. She was tall and thin. Wisps of white hair were caught up in a bun; a typical school mistress. During the war, she had fallen in love with Ted, a dashing pilot. They were about to marry when he got shot down over Germany. She waited and waited; he never came back. She devoted herself to teaching, knowing she would never marry and certainly never have children.

She had read an article in the daily paper about the terrible plight of the aborigine in Australia, and in Arnhem Land in the Northern Territory where she knew she was needed to teach these people. She had sold her furniture and belongings; her house in Newbury already was sold. Now she would devote herself to her mission. For the first time for many years, Ted had left her heart and mind. She thought this is truly what I want to do.

Strolling around the deck being admired by the ladies, Fred felt elated that they were looking at his big manly form. He liked to go down to the swimming pool sun bathe and sometimes, shadow box; he looked back at his climb to fame. An unknown young man from Camberwell, they called him the Beast from Camberwell when he was in the ring wrestling. Now he was at the top of his game and needed a break and also have a look at Australia's Surfers Paradise. There's money to be made in an up and coming sea side town. *It's going places, I want to be there.*

"Hello, handsome."

Ethel looked him up and down. *Mi. oh mi, one night with him. That's a real man!*

"Hello. Oh, hello, what's a good-looking lady like you doing all alone, no man, eh? I could help you out."

Ethel blushed. Ethel was all a tither; they settled down next to each other while sitting on the edge of the pool. Ethel was making Fred very sure she was interested in him by brushing his hairy arms with her hands, Eventually, Fred realised this was an opportunity not to miss and they slipped off to his cabin; oh yes, just to get to know each other just that little bit better.

Stella was waiting in their cabin, combing her lustrous brown long hair and drumming her fingers from time to time. She was waiting for her brother, Simon. She felt somewhat cross with Simon, but, for what? Anyway, here they both were on a round the world cruise.

They both had saved up enough money to treat themselves after both working so very hard. Simon as a waiter in a New York restaurant and she in a department store on the cosmetic counter; she hated some of those rich-old bitches swanning about, trying on lipstick and perfumes, but, here they were. Both could pretend to be rich now

On their table, at dinner, the boys were sitting next to Parul then Sutra, Dennis and Fred Lear. Opposite Fred Lear was Ethel and Benny Handeiside; she was a rather blousy woman with her hair tinted blond along with her husband. *Very effeminate,* Parul thought.

Parul noticed that Ethel kept looking over to Fred and to Parul; she thought that both were silently conversing in nods and winks. Something is going on there no doubt. Then, Ethel dropped her knife on the floor quickly picking it up and giving Fred another of her very wide smiles. Miss Amelia Stamp sat next to Benny. Benny was deep in conversation with her trying so hard to seem intelligent but failing badly. Then David Pickle, a thin good-looking young man, constantly looking over to the other table at a very beautiful young woman and her mother, who seemed very prim and proper a lady of breeding she thought.

The two young ones were in love, she thought. He was blushing, she was confident of herself; neither of them could keep their eyes off each other.

The evening came. Ethel had settled down in one of the wooden deck chairs, knitting, with a cup of beef tea. She thought it would be a good idea to try to finish of the sleeves of Bennies jersey. She only had a few more inches to go before she would finish the whole jersey.

I think I might stitch it all together this evening, she said to herself; then a stray thought came into her head. *Fred. dear. What a man, so tender.* If she had only met him before marrying Benny. What a man Fred is. She then started knitting again and taking sips of the beef tea which was so nice and warm.

The young ones were spinning around the dance floor. His hand around her small waist; he felt as if she were a small bird and one squeeze could break her wing.

Her mouth was inviting. Her lips parted. He could see her perfectly formed tongue. He felt completely entranced.

"Shall we go outside, Dolly, and watch the night sky?"

They walked out, hand in hand. By the ships railing, he stole a kiss, then another and continued on.

"What was that, Dolly?"

"I heard it too. Was it a scream, Dennis?"

"Don't know; I love you."

He curled her hair around one of his fingers, "I love you too, David. This is real, isn't it?"

"Yes. Yes."

Then, they both fell in to each other's arms again, and a scuffling noise was heard again.

"What, David?"

"I heard it too, Dolly. Come on, let's find out what it is."

Amelia heard a strange noise. It sounded like a cup smashing and then someone bashed in to her; the hood fell off, and she couldn't tell who it was; was it a female?

"Cameron."

'Yes, mi duck?"

"I'm going on to the deck, I want to see Ethel, I thought I would knit you a jersey too, I'll get the knitting pattern from her."

She went outside. The air was still. She could see Ethel sitting in her deck chair looking as if she was asleep; she was about to go back down stairs when she thought she heard a scuffling noise. She thought, maybe Ethel was now waking up; she walked over to her, saw a terrible sight, then screamed and ran.

Parul heard the scream and then running out on to the deck, Helen ran in to her arms.

"Oh my god, don't look. It's horrible," she cried and wailed.

"What do you mean, Mrs Mac Clures?"

Parul seemed a bit puzzled.

"She's there; Oh. Poor woman, it's horrible."

This time, Helen said this statement shouting. The young one's came around the corner.

"We heard a scream," both exclaimed.

Amelia ran in to Parul, both women nearly falling over, "I saw! The hood. Oh my God? Oh my God!"

Then Amelia carried on running around to the other side of the ship.

Earlier, just as she was coming out of her cabin to go upstairs to see the coming night, she noticed the young

American girl going in to her and her brothers' cabin and then almost straight away coming out.

"Filthy bastard. You arse. You leave him alone and get out. Go on, get."

Amelia could now see in to the cabin; and there, in the bed, naked, were two men. One was the American girl's brother, Simon with Benny, Mrs Handeiside's husband on top.

The young woman screamed more abuse at Benny, slapping him around the face.

"Get out. Out."

Benny, naked, grabbed his clothes and ran out, rubbing his face.

Amelia carried on walking, not wishing to see any more and just tut-tutting to herself.

Parul was now standing over the body. Three knitting needles were protruding out of Ethel's chest. Two had entered her body with such force that they had gone right up to the end of the needle. The other was half way through. A cup was smashed at the right side of her foot and it looked as if her watch had been torn off in the struggle and been smashed too. Not much blood, which seemed rather strange to Parul at the time and everything was wrong. There was something not right with this murder. *What was it?* Parul couldn't work it out.

Chapter 4

The more Parul looked at the scene of the crime, the more she felt something was not quite right; but what? Parul mused about this and that. Then, Sutra turned up with Dennis and the boys. When Dennis saw the dead body, he tried to usher the boys away but not before Michael having seen the body of the dead woman said out loud.

"Dad, she must be dead and why has she got knitting needles in her chest?"

Don tried to push past and have a better look, "Come on, boys, we are going to play chess downstairs."

"But, Dad! Dad! She's not."

Dennis cut Don short in the middle of him chattering, "Come on, you two, down stairs."

This time he sounded a bit firmer, "Dennis."

"Yes, Parul."

"Could you find Mr Handeisides and bring him up here?"

"Yes! Once I've got these two settled."

"Downstairs, come along! Come along, you've seen as much as you are going to see, I will not tell you again; do as I say."

Very reluctantly, he managed to walk the boys through the main slip doors off of the deck and down to the library.

Sutra stood looking at the poor woman.

"It's not quite right, Parul."

"I know; there is something not quite right about this; it almost looks like a stage set up. Everything is set out as if it were planned. Don't you see, Sutra?"

"Oh. Yes, I see; the cup is smashed on her right; wasn't she left-handed? Parul, you remember at dinner she dropped her knife on the floor and picked it up with her left hand? If she were right-handed, she wouldn't have picked it up, would she? Yes. Yes."

She said to herself out loud, "And look at the needles. Two stabbed in with hatred, the other not so much, almost makes you think. Yes."

"I see what you mean."

"What about the watch?"

She picked it up and the glass from the dial fell to the floor with a small clatter,

"Sutra, do you see the force that shattered the watch? It stopped it at 6:14 P.M.; the sun would still be up; well, at least we know when she was killed, don't we?"

Both ladies carried on looking at the body when the doctor turned up.

Helen, her husband and Fred Lear turned up. As soon as Fred saw Ethel, he sank to his knees, shaking, "Eth! Oh, Eth! You poor cow, what sod did this to you, my dear!"

At that, Fred broke down with tears spilling down his cheeks. The big man had been brought down like a tree that had suddenly been felled.

Parul noted the doctor was just slightly drunk with a cigarette dangling from his lips. He smelt of alcohol.

"What have we here?"

Arthur flicked his cigarette over the side in to the sea and he made a loud belch.

Arthur Bates, in his younger days, had passed through medical school with wonderful ideas set to spread his wings and make a name for himself in some practice.

But here he was, a ship's doctor, drinking heavily most nights.

He remembered when he had asked her to marry him and her refusal that dashed his hopes of everything. His dreams; oh and how he loved her.

"Is that her watch? She died at 6:14 P.M. and quite a struggle too!"

Now, the captain turned up. William Frazer was known as Willy to his crew. He was a very friendly man from Glasgow,

Scotland; he was slightly plump but quite a good-looking man in his younger days.

Willy faced Arthur, "Arthur, when did she die?"

"6:14 P.M., Willy."

"Um, I see. So, what do you think, Arthur? We are much too far to turn back or vie to somewhere else. We are right in the middle of the Indian ocean and our next stop is Freemantle. We'll have to put her on ice. I've already contacted the police there; so, let's get as many facts as we can."

"May I be of help? This doesn't seem to me to be a for gone conclusion, I think. Willy saw an Indian woman walk through the crowd of onlookers."

"And your name is?"

"Parul Das; and this is my aunty, Sutra Das."

"This is very unpleasant, Captain," Sutra said quite angrily.

"Quite so. It is a very nasty business. There really is not much I can do until we get to land."

"Yes. Yes. Captain."

"And that was our travelling companion, Mr Galvin."

As he ushered his children out of sight.

"I am a doctor, Captain."

"Well, would you be able to help, Arthur? Oh, I mean the doctor. He isn't. Let's say, not the best at present; would you take charge Miss Das?"

"Most certainly."

After bumping in to the Indian woman, Amelia ran around to the other side of the vessel. Towards the bow of the vessel, she could just make out the young American couple, leaning on the rails looking over the side of the boat. As she got closer, she could see both of them smoking cigarettes and loudly shouting at each other. As soon as they saw her running towards them, they stopped shouting.

"Hello."

"You should see that poor lady."

Half spluttered out and crying, Amelia tried to explain to them what she had seen.

"It was horrible; oh that poor woman."

Stella put her arm around Amelia's shoulder and slowly ushered her inside.

"Come on, honey. You need a slug of whiskey to calm you down."

She walked poor Amelia down to the bar on the next deck, followed by her brother.

After Dennis sorted out Don and Michael in the library, both had settled down with Bella, a rather pretty, golden-haired girl about two years older than themselves. All three were trying to play chess. It wasn't what either boy wanted to do; both were trying hard to impress Bella. She realised this was playing one boy against the other, and at last, both boys fell in to a shouting match then a fight started. Michael was, by now, on top of his brother trying to throttle his brother. Neither boys realised that Bella had turned her back on both. Laughing to herself as she skipped away, she left the boys to sort their differences out.

"She's gone, Micky."

"I'm sorry; um, girls?"

"Um, girls; I'm sorry too."

"Shake! Mates."

"We're mates; Micky, let's play chess."

"OK, Don."

Dennis walked up one floor to the next deck where he saw Mrs Handeisides's husband at the bar drinking. It looked as if he'd been drinking very heavily as he had several empty glasses around him; Dennis could see a cigarette tray full of cigarette butts.

"Um, I think you'd better come upstairs; your wife, has had a…"

At that moment, Amelia and the American young couple came in to the bar almost face-to-face with Dennis and Benny.

"You!" Stella spat at Benny; almost like a snake, while slipping her other arm over her brother's shoulder.

Benny stepped back as if he were about to be bitten.

"That's enough, young lady."

Dennis felt that he certainly didn't want an argument now; so, he moved Benny around the very cross-young lady up the stairs to the deck where Benny's wife lay dead.

"Eth what! What! Oh my god."

Parul saw Mrs Handeisides's husband half running; then stopping and running again till he came to his wife's body.

Behind him came Dennis, Amelia and the two Americans.

Sutra saw the young American woman stop; then, putting her hand over her mouth, reaching and then coiling herself in to her brother's shoulder.

"Oh god. Oh god. What. How? Who? Oh god! She's? Is she?"

All this was half screamed, half begging loudly and very dramatic; Benny sank to his knees crying, wailing.

What a picture to be upheld. All circled around the dead body.

Sutra very gently put her arm around the young man slowly, edging him away.

"Come on. There! There! Stop crying."

She took Benny down to his cabin and sat with him while he curled up on his bed weeping.

Later, the captain arranged for two seamen to pick the body up and take it down to the ship's freezer; the small crowd slowly broke away going in their different directions leaving Parul and Dennis standing at the railings looking out at the moon and stars. What a night and how lovely it was. Now everything had changed. There had been a gruesome murder, yet, the night was benign; still and so beautiful.

Parul looked at Dennis; he put his arm around her. She shivered and started very softly crying, "Dennis, that poor woman!"

He very lightly brushed a stray lock of hair from her face and kept his hand on her cheek and very softly uttered, "Yes."

Both stood looking out at the beauty of the night; a star flashed across the heavens.

"I care for you so much."

"I know, Dennis."

Both were so close and almost kissed; but not quite yet; both wanted to, yet, both were afraid. Dennis brought her hand up to his lips and kissed it tenderly; she felt an explosion in her throat. She wanted to swallow and get it out of the way; yet, to keep it there and! And! Then, both turned to the night sky. The black sea softy splashed up against the mighty ship as she sped her human cargo to a new life; a new beginning, a new hope. Love. And so much hate.

Chapter 5

All three sat at breakfast very quiet. Don and Michael had eaten their breakfast very hurriedly and gone off to play with Bella, who, had been eating her breakfast at the next table with her parents. She had seen the two Indian twins and poked her tongue out at them. Don had put both his hands up to his ears and waved them at her whilst poking his tongue out too. The three children then ran off to play. Leaving the three adults musing over their half-eaten boiled eggs. The waiter broke the silence.

"Would you like some tea or coffee?"

"Tea for us, please."

"I'll try coffee."

"Sutra, coffee?"

"Parul, sometimes. I will try something different."

Dennis just looked on at both women.

"Thank you, young man."

Sutra took the coffee from the waiter, looked deep in to its black swirling depths and pondered on nothing; taking a sip he said, "Eee, that's sour."

Then taking more sips, "Do you like it, Sutra?"

"Do you know? I'm not sure, Dennis, it's sour yet it's clearing my head and I'm not sure; but I think I like it. You too should try it."

"Not me, Aunty."

"I'd much rather have tea too then."

"You don't know, Dennis, till you've tried it; go on, have a sip."

"OK; just one."

As he sipped, he turned his nose up at it, "No. No. It's tea for me."

"I tried it some years ago. I don't like the flavour at all; give me tea."

"Well, you are both missing something. I wouldn't have believed it, but, it's clearing my head and I feel quite good; very bright too. Why don't we lay things out? We have a murder; a very nasty one! Somebody hated her very much. We need to sort out a few possibilities, don't we? Three needles, one person or three; why? We've got a few weeks before we get to Freemantle."

"The Australian police will take over. I agree, Sutra; we three have enough time to try and sort out what has happened.

Dennis spoke, "What do you think, Parul?"

"That sounds OK to me, Dennis."

Sutra sipped her new found concoction while the other two huddled together over the table mapping out the murder.

"I can't get it out of my head; the whole thing is staged, isn't it? Whoever did this is trying to make it look as if she fought; but she didn't; she was asleep, yet, she would have woken up if…"

"Parul, if she were drugged, she wouldn't, would she?"

"Now, Sutra, you've opened a whole can of worms there!"

"Yes, I know, Dennis but."

Parul sat listening to both Dennis and Sutra discussing their new ideas.

Then he spoke to both of them, "Do you realise what this means?"

"What?" both exclaimed.

"This means more killers; Sutra, how many?"

"Oh, dear me, you're right, my dear; oh dear, why don't we say everyone on this ship could have an alibi, couldn't they? Well, we've got to set this all out then talk to as many possible people that may well be involved. That Scottish women found the body," Dennis said.

"No, wasn't it that English school teacher?"

Parul thought for a few moments and then replied to Dennis, "Do you know, Dennis; I think it was! Why don't we interview both women, then her husband, the young Americans and so on?"

All three set out who they would individually interview and then get back for a debriefing later in the library.

Sutra had the Scottish couple and the school mistress while Parul had the American brother and sister, the mother and daughter and the young man who was sweet on the young woman.

Dennis took up the rest of the slack with Mr Handeisides; he had stated he thought it might be a better idea for him to talk to the young man who was quite over the top with his flamboyant effeminacy and the doctor but he would wait till he was sober.

"I'll also talk to that wrestler. There was something going on between him and the dead woman wasn't there."

"He was very upset." Sutra made this statement whilst rubbing her chin and wagging her head from side to side.

Later, Dennis saw Fred Lear on the upper deck, smoking a cigarette gazing over the side of the ship looking at the waves.

"Hello."

Fred suddenly looked around after wiping a tear off his cheek.

"You startled me. Nasty business; we only just met; fine woman, fine woman. Oh, yes, I thought I'd found her; my, Oh God, I'll never see her again. Oh my God."

"You just met her on board?"

"Yes."

Dennis thought about his next question. He needed to find out as much as he could about Fred.

"Was she?"

"Look, cock, I've been wrestling all my adult life; me dear old mum gave me a posh name Frederick. As I grew up, all the kids made fun of me posh name so I had to grow up quick and being a big bloke, I learnt how to look after me self, so I went in to the ring and rose through the ranks. Now, I'm a top dog and on me way to Aussie; then I met her. It was a quick romp, but, afterwards, we talked, and I could see a future with her. Her on me arm. Oh blimey, what now? It's all stuffed, mate! Bloody stuffed, what now? We've got to get the arsehole who did this to her. If I find out who he is, I'll kill him. I'll kill him. The bastard."

After a while, he calmed down.

"Where were you around say about 6:15 or before, Mr Lear?"

After taking a large handkerchief out of his pocket and blowing very hard, he cleared his nose and throat.

"If I remember, around about 6ish, I bumped in to that bleeding twit. That twit of a husband knocked in to me; he was in such a rush flying, around the corner. Someone had given him a right smack; his face was so red and he was trying to tuck his shirt into his pants. Didn't see me coming at all; He kind of looked at me and then carried on to the bar; he's a right gormless burk! By the time he turned to go, it would be 6:10 or about. Then, I heard a scream and went to investigate. Got on to the upper deck, saw a commotion and then her; yeah her!"

Then he started crying again and turned to the waves not wanting anyone to see his grief.

Dennis turned to go inside; he felt a sudden chill and shivered; yet, it wasn't cold nor windy, but a beautiful morning.

Dennis noticed Benny. He sat there looking out to sea with a blank look on his face.

"Can I ask you a few questions about the time of the murder, Mr Handiesides? What were you doing at 6:15 P.M.?"

"This." Pointing to his now quite red face and a black eye.

Benny told Dennis the whole story. The fight and being caught by Stella, in a rather compromising situation with her brother and slapping him around the face and Amelia popping her head around the door of the cabin then walking away. Then, he shrugged his shoulders and looked quite sad.

"She's dead; that's all that I care about."

He turned back to the sea and Dennis could see he wasn't going to get much else from him and so, he walked back inside.

Sutra was sitting in the library about 10 in the morning, sipping her by now usual cup of black coffee with just one teaspoon of brown sugar when the Scottish couple walked past.

"Morning."

"Morning to you too."

She moved over and beckoned them to sit with her.

"Been on cruises before?"

"No, we are going to see our son and new baby in Australia. I'm Helen and this is my husband Cameron."

"What about you?"

"It's a long story and now my niece is trying to find out what's going on with this terrible murder. Where were you two about 6:15?"

"We were both in our cabin."

Helen interrupted her husband, "Then I went upstairs. I wanted to have a word with the dead, err, I mean, err, the American woman. She was knitting a jersey for her husband and I thought I'd knit one for Cameron; I needed a pattern and asked if she had any extra wool. Maybe, I could start while we are on board. I went outside and saw her asleep in her deck chair, I nearly turned around to go back down stairs; then, I looked again; she looked so still and I saw her cup on the deck smashed; so, thinking she might be sick or something, I walked up to her then I saw the needles. I screamed and ran and then bumped into your niece, poor woman."

"There, there, me duck," as he put his arm around his very softly weeping wife.

"What time was that?" Sutra asked.

Through tears and sniffing, Helen spluttered, "6:20-ish."

"Whoever could do a thing like that needs to be strung up; that's what I say."

Then, Cameron very tenderly kissed the forehead of his wife.

"Thank you so much; you both have been so helpful. I do hope we find who's done this crime."

"I just hope we do; she was so nice; really good at knitting." Helen said and she shuddered. With a helping arm from her husband, they got up and walked away.

Sutra, after writing all this down on a pad, went for a stroll along the deck.

Sutra watched the flying fish darting this way and that and thinking, *who could have done this, I wonder?* She saw the school mistress walking towards her.

"Hello." both ladies exclaimed to each other.

"Shall we find some where that's not quite so windy and have a chat, Miss Stamp?"

"Oh yes, that would be nice."

So, Sutra ushered Amelia in front of her inside the lounge and both sat down.

A waiter came to their table

"Yes, ladies, what would you like?"

Sutra recognised him as the waiter that had introduced her to coffee.

Miss Stamp addressed the waiter, "Could I have tea please? What are you going to have Miss Das? Will you join me?"

Without Sutra saying a word, the waiter leaned over towards Sutra, "Would madam like her usual?"

"You know my weakness."

Sutra almost purred out her request and gave him one of her radiant smiles. Sutra needed to ask Miss Stamp some questions.

"Tell me, what you know?"

"Do call me Amelia."

Sutra sat back whilst Amelia went on and on about her entire life story and at one point, she almost fell asleep.

"I'm not boring you."

As Sutra awoke with a splutter, "Oh! No! Oh no! I'm just relaxing my eyes." She felt she needed to prop her eye lids open with match sticks.

"Go on, go on, it's so interesting," she said as she took a big swig out of her coffee cup and drained it.

"Would madam like another coffee?" he said smiling from ear to ear.

"Yes, make it a big one this time. I think I'm going to need it."

Amelia carried on until she came to the night of the murder and telling Sutra as much as she could think of.

"Was there anything unusual after you saw the murdered woman, Amelia?"

"As I ran around the deck, someone bumped in to me. I've no idea who it was."

"You don't, Amelia?"

"No. Oh, his hood fell off."

At that moment, the American woman passed by.

"Oh, hello, I hope you're treating our school teacher right?"

"Yes! Yes, we are very slowly interviewing as many as we think may be able to help us piece together that night."

The American young woman gave both ladies a brilliant smile as she walked away smoking.

Amelia waved her hand back and forwards, "That's a very nasty habit, I hate smoking."

"Yes. I do too."

"I'm feeling a bit tired; I think I'll go lay down in my cabin. This sort of nasty thing is very draining, isn't it, Miss Das?"

"Yes, oh yes."

Amelia carried on to the staircase and walked out of Sutra's sight.

As Amelia walked down the stairs to her cabin, she came across Stella, smoking in the foyer. Then, both ladies went down the stairs together, talking of this and that, as they bumped in to Dolly.

"Are you all right? You look a bit pale."

"Yes, I've a bit of a headache, young lady; I'm going to try to sleep it off. All this nasty affair is so upsetting."

"I'll pop down later to see how you are."

"You're very sweet, dear."

"Yes, she does look a bit under the weather."

Dolly could see that Stella looked really concerned and Amelia did not look good.

"See you later."

"Not to worry, Dolly. I'll tuck her up in bed."

Dolly turned around and carried on back upstairs leaving Stella to help Amelia.

Stella ushered Amelia into Amelia's cabin and on to her bed.

"Honey, have you any aspirins?"

"Yes, in my hand bag on the chair."

"Here, honey. Just two."

"That should be enough to get me to sleep." Stella made sure Amelia took the aspirins before she left. Closing the door of the cabin, she walked back upstairs.

Amelia lay there for some time. Her mind travelled to her lovely airman. She could see his blond curls as he waved goodbye for the last time. She then fell into a deep sleep.

Then, she awoke. What was that noise outside her cabin? *No. No.* She assured herself. It was nothing. Then she fell off to sleep again.

Waking again, she felt a pressure on her face heavier and heavier. She couldn't breathe. She flayed this way and that trying to release the pressure of the pillow. She ripped at the pillow. She tried to scratch her attacker, but, the pressure of the pillow was heavy. She was falling, falling slower and slower, slower. Then blackness and nothing.

Dennis was strolling around the ship with Parul; they took in the salty breeze. The wind, though not too strong, buffeted them around. They sought shelter in the bar though neither of them drunk alcohol.

There slouched at the bar was the doctor, drunk.

"Hellooo, you two."

His eyes were red and he had an ash tray of spent cigarettes and one dangling from his fingers.

"Have a drinksy; I won't bite well, not now," as Arthur almost fell off the stool he was sitting on.

"Sorry, I'm a bit tiddly; don't say no pretty lady; she said no. I loved her. I wanted to marry her?" Arthur was now very drunk.

As he said this, tears ran down his booze-stricken face.

"I loved her; I really did. Now. Oh dear. Oh dear, so wees having a drinksy."

This time, he completely fell off the stool on to the floor and passed out. The barman leaned over the bar; seeing poor old Arthur on the floor signalled a very tall somewhat camp waiter.

"George?"

"Yes, your highness?"

"Cut the wit, George! Pick him up and take him to his cabin, will you?" the barman snarled.

"Anything for you!" he said as he gave the barman a wink and a kiss.

"George, cut the cackle and pick him up."

"Yes, sir."

As he saluted the barman, he then picked the bundle up as if it were dirty washing down to his cabin.

Both looked at each other. Parul giggled and Dennis patted her on the head.

She, taking his hand off her head, gave a very deep curtsy, "My lord."

"Stop it. You're getting very cheeky, young lady."

"Oh, yes."

"Yes."

"Well, Dennis, that's one possible murderer we can strike off our list. He would never be sober to do a single thing."

"So true."

"Poor devil; he must have been jilted when he was younger, Parul."

"Dennis, that's true."

They thought no more about it. They went back outside. After watching the waves cresting and smashing up against the ship, Parul left Dennis to go inside.

"I think I'll go inside for a bit, Dennis."

"I'll stay and do a bit of thinking. Bye, see you later, Parul."

As Parul was walking, she passed the entrance to the bar, and saw the young American brother and sister sitting in the lounge having a coffee and both in a haze of smoke. They were signalling Parul to join them.

"May I join you?"

"Sure, honey, come and sit between us. Simon, pull your chair back and let Miss Das in."

"Oh, call me Parul. Can I ask you a few questions about the time of the murder?"

"Sure."

Parul was hoping the young American woman would be able to tell her as much information as she could.

Stella spoke and informed Parul of the fight, slapping Mrs Handeisides husband around the face after finding him with Simon in their cabin. Simon looked quite embarrassed about the graphic detail that his sister went into hanging his head rather low.

"That school mistress saw almost everything."

Simon saying this and if anything, his head seemed lower. Parul couldn't help but feel sorry for him, as his sister was carrying on berating him for his stupidity.

"Well, thank you so much."

She got up and headed for the bar where she saw Lady Perrin and her daughter; she was staring in to the young English man's eyes. He too was staring at her. She noted they held each other's hands under the table.

"Hello, do sit down. Try this Gin and Tonic, it's so good. The barman has mixed it just right."

Lady Perrin took small sips as if it were nectar of the gods.

"This dreadful business and that poor woman; the whole thing is just beyond belief."

"Oh, yes, I do agree. Did you and your daughter see anything?"

"We were in the ballroom dancing."

With that statement, Dolly started to giggle.

"Goodness, my girl, do behave, this is quite a dreadful matter. And David, you should know better. I do believe your leading her on. Now, both of you concentrate!"

Parul noted that, this time, Lady Perrin was glaring at David and David was completely ignoring her fop which she looked even more cross.

"Anyway, as I was saying, we were in the ballroom dancing; I was dancing with the most beautiful girl on board."

He brushed a lock of hair from her face and she kissed his hand.

"Err, erm, you two, stop it, stop it; look we're being stared at."

David cut her short again. Lady Perrin was fuming now.

"We heard a scream."

"No, darling; we went outside first and you kissed me. Then we heard the scream. Then we kissed again."

"Get on with it without the—"

This time, Dolly cut her mother short.

"As I was saying, you said you loved me, David."

"Yes, I did; then we heard a funny sort of noise and so, we went to investigate; but wasn't the noise first, before the scream?"

"David, do you know, I'm not sure now. Anyway, we came around the corner and saw you standing over the body."

"When did you hear the scream?"

Both looked at each other.

"6:15 P.M.," both exclaimed and nodded.

"I must go, Mum; I promised that school mistress I would call her in her cabin. She looked quite sick; she was with the American woman."

"Yes, my dear, I must go too."

All three headed for the school mistress cabin after saying their farewell to Parul.

Chapter 6

As they walked down the staircase, Dolly just chatted to her mother, "She's very nice, isn't she, mum?"

"That Indian woman. Has quite a bit of class, wouldn't you say, David?"

"Yes, Mrs P."

His quip made Gwen really angry. David never took things seriously, plus she still didn't like his attentions towards her daughter. She had better prospects on her mind for her and David was working class and wasn't, what she felt, her daughter should be looking for! So, this silly quip, though not truly important, really got under her skin. She also felt David knew he was upsetting her; that fact made her more cross. He was a silly stupid boy.

"Dolly, darling pop, see how she is? Look, the door's open."

"OK, Mother."

She stepped through into Amelia's cabin. She screamed. There was Amelia with a ripped pillow over her face. Amelia had tried in vain to rip the pillow from her face. Screaming again, she ran out of the cabin in to the arms of her mother.

"What's up, darling?"

Gwen hugged her daughter for a while, as she stroked her hair and slowly getting her calm enough to leave her with David, so that she too could look inside the cabin. What she saw inside rocked her.

"Ee wot a t' do, another murder? Come here, pet, let me give you a cuddle. Ee by gum lass, Davy lad, get the captain, the doctor; Ee wot a mess. Come on, mi pet, stop blathering, muther's here. I'll not let anything happin ta ya. Go, son, make it sharpish; go on ya good lad!"

David was taken back by Gwen's sudden slip in to her Yorkshire accent as much as the new murder, and when Gwen had told him to get the captain and doctor, he hesitated as Gwen took him in to her arms as well. All three hugged.

"Off ya go, lad."

David left the two women hugging and weeping.

David ran into the captain spluttering out what had happened. Both went to find the doctor.

They found Arthur in his cabin completely drunk with one empty bottle of rum in his arm's as if cradling a baby. Both then went looking for Parul and her two sidekicks.

The captain looked very stern at Parul.

"There's another murder; you'd better come and see. It's the school mistress this time."

Sutra looked at both Parul and Dennis and exclaimed,

"That's put the cat amongst the pigeons, hasn't it?"

All five stood for a moment then went to Amelia's cabin.

There, they found Dolly and her mother outside the cabin in each other's arms weeping.

"It's horrid in there."

This time, Gwen had gathered herself together and regained her lady-like composure and perfect diction; then once again she slipped into her Yorkshire accent.

"Wot a ta do. Mi dear pet." All the while, she was stroking her daughter's hair.

"Come here, lad. Come here."

Enfolding both Dolly and David in her arms, David felt tears spilling down his face and he hugged Gwen even harder. He had never felt this genuine affection before and he felt he needed to alter his opinion of Gwen. Maybe she isn't quite such a stuck-up old fart as he had first thought and may be, just maybe, he felt a spark of understanding her. Well, she was only looking after her daughter's best interest; so, he realised he would have to start to treat her with a bit more respect and perhaps stop taking the rise out of her. She wasn't such a bad old duck after all and he smiled to himself. All of them stood looking at the murdered woman and her futile effort in attempting to rip the pillow from her face. Then, Sutra noticed there was one very small spot of blood on the white sheet that Amelia had tangled in one of her hands; it was slightly smeared and one more spot on the pillow.

"She put up quite a fight and she scratched her murderer So now we are looking for someone with a scratch."

"Yes, Sutra, that's true; that may not be at all as easy as you may think."

"That's true, Dennis."

"Parul, you've said nothing so far."

"Yes, I know. I'm thinking this murder makes all of our investigations null and void, doesn't it? Because what can possibly link both murders."

"I hope you three can untangle all of this because I can't and we are now only four days from Freemantle. I'll put the body in with the other one till we get to Australia. Then it'll be up to the Australian police to sort it out."

Parul hardly heard this statement from the captain because there was something, an idea in her head something that was tickling her thoughts. What if Amelia had witnessed the first murder. She would have to be silenced, *Yes, oh, yes!*

She said these two words to herself, but out loud.

"Pardon, Miss Das?"

"Oh, don't mind me, captain, I was thinking out loud."

But she knew she needed to tell both Dennis and Sutra as soon as she could of her assumptions.

"Would you mind, just say an hour, letting us three look around the cabin before you take the body away captain?"

"Certainly, young lady."

The captain left and went off to sort out the seamen to take the body away leaving the very silent three looking at the whole murder scene.

Lady Perrin gathered up her two young ones. Thought it would be a good idea to get up on to the deck and sit in the sun, with Dolly and David. *Yes. May be the lads not too bad.* She had noticed he too had wept. *He can't be such a bad lad after all; maybe I'll need to think more about this young chap, maybe.* Then she felt a tear going down her face.

She remembered many years ago, before Dolly came in to her and her husband's world, a little boy. A bright and happy child. Then only too soon. He was taken from them. *Maybe, yes, maybe, I've found mi bright eyed son, mi apple of mi eye.* As she held David even closer and kissed his hair.

All three detectives stood at the railings staring out to sea. Looking at what? Nothing; nothing at all except the sun the wind and the sea and a bond between them all.

"What's the time Dennis?"

Looking at his watch for a moment.

"It's 11:37 A.M., Parul. The English lady with her daughter and the English young man, David, discovered the body first. I'll find out what time they discovered the body."

After what seemed a long time Dennis spoke again.

"I've got an idea; shoot me if you want both of you, but, I think there is a link here."

Parul and Sutra nodded.

Then a long silence again.

"She knew something, didn't she?"

"Mm." Sutra said whilst stroking her chin.

"We've got a very nasty business on our hands; so, what do we do now?"

As she started to look around the cabin, looking at letters, papers and passports; anything that might help them sort this out. Dennis and Parul were helping her. All three mindlessly sifting through the poor murdered victim's belongings and coming up with nothing at all. Just the ripped pillow now taken away from Amelia's face and the blood and flesh under one of her fingernails.

"She knew her murderer."

Sutra stated whilst shaking her head from side to side.

"There's nothing here, but, some poor woman that knew much too much. Shall we go? There is no more to be done. We need to sit down somewhere."

Dennis and Parul nodded in agreement. They all left the crime scene.

They went to the library saying nothing.

Then Dennis chirped, "This is by far more complicated, isn't it? She saw the first murder, that I'm quite sure of, so, the murderer had to silence her."

"Don't sound so defeated, Dennis; I realise it's not just one murder but two; but now we know that she scratched her murderer, didn't she? All we need to do is find someone with a scratch on their arm or someplace else; neck? Face? Could it be more than one murderer?"

Parul thought about Dennis's statement and nodded at him.

"Yes, Dennis, you could be right," Sutra stated.

"You two have forgotten one thing. Well, maybe three, there were three knitting needles in Mrs Handeisides chest weren't there, so, three murderers. What do you both think about that?" Dennis chirped in rather cheekily.

"Oh, boy, Sutra, that's true; you are not just a pretty face, are you?" Sutra replied.

"Very funny, Dennis."

Her smile wasn't exactly an amused smile.

Dennis was quiet again, thinking and trying to clear his mind.

Parul mapped out what they were all thinking.

"We all agree that the first murder was committed by three murderers. The second, by one; maybe with an accomplice keeping an eye out? Just in case they were disturbed. Now we know we need to interview every one again, except for the doctor. Throughout this whole business, he's been drunk."

Sutra thought about what Parul had just said about the doctor. "How do we know he was drunk?"

Dennis sat back in his chair. "Sutra's right, you know, Parul! How do we know he was drunk all the time? That makes more complications now."

Parul thought about this and a sort of scenario was taking place in her mind; but who or whom could/would do this sort of thing? What motive and so much hate?

All three discussed this in length, putting first one possibility then another and all still coming back to the same thought, someone must have hated Mrs Handeiside's enough to plan this all out; the evening was closing in, so, all three went to their cabins to shower and get changed for dinner. Dennis got the boys organised and dressed.

The three stepped out on to the passageway to go to dinner. As they turned the corner to go up the stairwell, there was Parul and Sutra. Parul was wearing a light red with gold flowers swirling in intricate patterned sari with a very light gold silk scarf draped around her neck and shoulders; Sutra, a green and silver one; just as dazzling and also with a silver scarf.

Dennis had never seen Parul wearing a sari before and the transformation was breath-taking. Her hair, though not very long, she had managed to sweep the sides up and the back had a very ornate mother of pearl hair clip in the shape of a butterfly in it. Also, regarding her make-up, she used a lipstick which she had always stated she never wore and didn't like at all; but, what a vision. He couldn't take his eyes off her.

"You can put your tongue in now." Sutra eyed both of them and shook her head back and forth.

"My, oh my. Looks to me, boys, we have the two most beautiful ladies on board this ship. Wow, aren't we lucky?"

As all five walked up the staircase to the dining room, and making their entrance, the two boys in front and Dennis with a lady on each arm.

The dinner was as usual very good. Superb in fact. They had their own table this time; everyone had their finery on this night as it was the captain's dinner.

After all the days of upset with the murders, this was a spectacular night. Almost everything seemed to be forgotten and everyone looked as if their troubles had passed.

Sutra had Lobster Thermador as a dish. She had never tried it before; both Parul and Dennis had steak; Diane and the boys had Spaghetti Carbonara.

Parul and Dennis's steak came to the table by a waiter who took great care and dramatic skill at cooking the meal at their table. At last, he lit the brandy in the pan to great excitement of the boys.

"Wow, look at the flames."

The whole thing was very spectacular. Then, Parul tried to show the boys how they should eat their spaghetti by using the spoon and fork rolling around the spaghetti in the spoon before putting it in to their mouths.

There was suddenly a commotion at the end of the dining room. From within the kitchen came a waiter with a cake with candles. The waiter held it high as he went passed their table to the other side where there was very excited little girl.

"Oh, Mummy. Oh, Mummy."

As the waiter set down the burning cake in front of her, he stood back to admire it.

"Do I blow the candles out, Daddy?"

"Well, it's your eleventh birthday, Tilly."

"OH. OH."

"Come on before they go out."

"Yes, Mummy."

As Tilly blew the candles out, everyone in the dining room sang.

"Happy birthday to you! Happy birthday to you! Happy birthday, dear Tilly; happy birthday to you!"

Then a loud hurray and everyone clapped.

"Did you see the boys? They nearly screwed their heads off trying to see who the birthday girl was, Dennis."

"Yes, I saw, Sutra."

The little girl and her parents were going around giving everyone a piece of cake. When they got to the boys table, the little girl said, "Mummy, I'll do this table."

The little girl had a blue and white dress with a big blue and white bow at the back of her hair.

She gave a low curtsy to the grownups and then started to give slices of cake out.

She turned to Don, "I've saved the biggest piece for you. My name's Tilly; what's yours?"

The boys sniggered; Michael pushed Don.

"Go on, Don."

Giving his brother another big jab, he said, "Go on, she's not going to bite." he sniggered again.

All the while, Tilly was fluttering her eye lids and sort of swirling her dress and every so often, the bow at the back of her head kept hitting Don on the nose.

Eventually, Don, giving out with a sneeze, replied, "Mine is Don."

As he wiped his nose, she danced off back to her table looking back every so often to make sure both boys were looking at her. She sat down with an ease of a temptress having won over her captured foe and humming to herself.

"Fancy having your birthday on a big ship? Your daddy and I love you very much, Tilly."

"Mum?"

"Yes, my darling?"

"When I'm grown up, I'm going to marry that boy."

"Are you?"

"Yes, Daddy, I am."

Her father looked at his wife.

"Looks to me, Jenny, as if our girls made her mind up."

"Well, Dale, she's a cut off the old block. If I remember, you said to me I'm going to marry you and that was when we first met. Do you remember, Dale?"

"How could I ever forget that music, and that Maori maiden in front of me? With those big brown eyes of yours, I knew I was going to marry you."

"Oh, Dale, my dear man and I suppose I fell for you too."

They both kissed over the table.

"My handsome man."

"My beautiful wife."

Chapter 7

The day dawned. The weather, the rain and wind. It seemed to match. The three detectives' mood too. All were sitting at the breakfast table after a night of splendour and happiness. And now that was forgotten; back to the problem and how to sort out what evidence they had so far gleaned from the passengers.

"This coffee isn't doing the trick this morning; I'm feeling quite yuck; my head's thick. I feel as if we are back to the beginning. How far have we really got? We have two murders; first one, three needles! Three murderers! Second murder, one to do the dirty deed, the other to keep watch and another to help hold the victim down because, even though the victim was from what the passport says born April the Second, 1921, she was a woman of about 49, 50. Though a slight frame, she would be fighting for her life. We know she scratched one of her murderers. So once again, we are looking at three murderers and one has a scratch on him or her."

After Sutra had given this long collection of facts, there was a long silence. They all looked out at the rain slashing up against the glass of the restaurant; boiling water from the kettle clouded up the inside of the window's near where the breakfast was laid out.

Lots of bustle was heard as the rest of the passengers piled their plates up with bacon, eggs, waffles, jam, marmalade, cornflakes and all sorts of breakfast delights on to each other's plates. Children were being told to sit, to stop running around and get your breakfast; sit still. The general hustle and bustle of breakfast. All this noise didn't seem to penetrate the three; everything seemed gloomy to them.

Finally, Dennis turned back to Sutra having stirred his tea so many times, it was now cold.

"I do agree, Sutra; with all you say. Now, just to remind us all and please don't think I'm being overly smart, I'm not, I'm trying to think practically. We only have a short time before we get to Australia; three days. What do you say, Parul, is it three days?"

Parul answered and almost said her statement to herself, as she drummed her fingers on the table like a drum.

"It must be such little time and as Sutra says, we are sort of back to the beginning. But we are not. We have all this information about all the people that we interview. The only one that we can scrub out completely is the doctor. He's always been far too drunk to think of him having anything to do with this whole matter. Could he be acting?"

Another long silence.

"Yes, that's possible, but, when we interviewed him, I don't think that could have been an act. Falling off of that stool and that waiter picking him up like a bag of dirty washing; oh no, that wasn't an act. So, we can definitely rule him out of having anything at all to do with this whole business? Now what?"

Parul thought for some moment before carrying on.

"Let's look at the first murder. We know the victim went up to the deck to do some knitting. She picked up a cup of beef tea; where did she get it from? The steward in the restaurant? We haven't found out which steward gave it to her; we need to first find out who he was. Then, she took it upstairs and settled herself to sipping it and carrying on with her knitting. I think a drug must have been put in to the drink, before she got it; either before or after, because, she didn't struggle. I know the doctor said she must have put up a big fight, but, if she were drugged first, she would be sitting there motionless seeing her murderers doing the stabbing and not being able to move or shout or scream. I'm going down to my cabin and looking up my medical books to remind myself of the medication that could be used. I'll be back, don't go away, you two."

"Ha! Ha! Parul, we will just sit here twiddling our thumbs, shall we?"

"Aunty, there's no need for sarcasm!"

"Parul, dear, it wasn't sarcasm, it's called desperation. What you are saying is, it must be the doctor and as Dennis said, it couldn't possibly be; but, drunks aren't drunk all the time; maybe he's drunk now because he killed her."

Parul had started to walk away. But after this, she turned back to face both of them.

"Um, yes."

"What, Parul? You said that almost as if you were saying it to yourself."

"Well, yes, aunty, I was sort of, I was thinking too. I'm sort of getting a picture in my mind; let me look in to my medical books."

She turned and sped down the stairs to her cabin, leaving Dennis and Sutra pondering what she had just discussed with them.

Dennis and Sutra sat there not saying too much; Sutra got another cup of coffee from her favourite waiter.

When he came back with her black elixir, Sutra looked up to his face.

"Would you mind me asking you a few questions? Who gives out the beef tea? Um, sorry, I don't know your name."

"Jonny Dunn. I know you are part of a team that's trying to sort out this nasty business, I'll help you all I can. I usually give out the beef tea and it was me who gave her a cup of beef tea. She had her knitting with her. She seemed a bit flustered, as she was trying to balance the cup while carrying the knitting. I carried on ladling out cups of beef tea, orange juice for the children, tea and coffee. I saw her put it down once, maybe twice, then she gathered up her knitting and carried on upstairs. It looked as if she were heading outside. Then, I gave that very good-looking American lady a cup of coffee. That's all I know."

"Did you see where the American lady went?"

"No, I'm sorry, lady, I did not. As I said, I carried on with my duty; true, that's all I know. I hope I've been helpful."

Sutra just nodded to him.

"Oh, sorry, Yes. You've been very helpful, and keep that coffee rolling. I'm becoming an addict."

Jonny gave her a big smile then turned to go back to the kitchen.

"I'm not sure, but I think I saw the American lady follow the old lady. OH, yes. She dropped her knitting, they almost collided."

"Well, what do you think of that, Dennis."

"Sutra, we had better talk to the American lady now."

"Yes. Yes."

She put her arm through his and they went to look for their victim.

The boys were playing Shuffle board when Tilly turned up with another little girl in tow.

"Hello, Don," she said whilst fluttering her eye lids.

"This is Barbara, my best friend."

"Hello, call me Badger. They all do at school. I have a pony called Muffin; he's brown and white and Daddy said they were shipping him over to New Zealand, so that, when we get to Timaru, Muffin will carry on to our new home. It's on I think the Canterbury Plains. It's Fairlie; Daddy's got a big lot of land there. Uncle Dick died and gave it to my daddy. Now, we are going there to live."

Badger carried on chattering about all her family history to Michael while her friend smooched around Don, asking him this question and that.

Eventually, Don thought it would be a good idea if he and his brother played shuffle board with the two girls. All four settled down to play.

Everything was going fine; all four children were having so much fun in each other's company until Bella came around the corner from sitting with her parents in the library. As soon as she saw the four having fun, and that very ugly posh freckle faced ginger haired little girl playing with Michael, she couldn't have that. She stormed in, as angry as she could possibly be and grabbed Badger's shuffle stick and threw it over board into the sea, and screamed out to Badger, who by now was crying.

"Your horrid little beast. He's my best friend! Keep away from him!"

Grabbing Michael's sleeve, she pulled him away from the group.

"Michael. Michael." She almost purred this statement out. "I thought you were my best friend."

Michael cut her off short, "Who said I was your best friend? Not me."

Bella stamped her foot and ran away crying.

"Well, Micky, you certainly can pick 'em."

"Donny, boy, we're mates?"

"Yes."

"I think she's nice but, Don? She wants to be with me all the time and split us up. Don't want that! Boy, she does get cross."

Tilly had been holding Badger and Badger had stopped crying, but only after several blows in her hanky.

"I'm not ugly, am I?"

This statement made her cry again; blowing her nose, her eyes were streaming.

"No. She's a horrid girl I'm telling my mummy, Badger."

Both girls walked away hand in hand with Badger still weeping.

"Well, Donny Boy, it's just me and you. Why do girls get so upset? We were only playing with the girls."

"I don't know; just think being married to them all the time; how do men put up with them? I'm not getting married ever. Ever."

"Me neither. They spoiled our game, who would want to be. Oh, girls. Yuk! Double yuk!"

"Yuk. Yuk. Treble Yuk!"

Both sniggered, then ran off to find some other game to play which didn't involve girls.

The boys eventually went to the library to play chess, which Dennis had after many efforts taught them to play and now, they were by far much better than him, but one very important reason why he'd taught them the game was so that it would help with their concentration.

And at present, both he and Sutra were concentrating on the murders. When the boys came into the library, they saw their dad and Sutra sitting staring out to sea, both with a very blank look on their faces.

"Donny boy, they look fed up."

"Yes, Micky. Dad and Sutra would be a lot happier if Parul and Dad were married."

"I love Parul, Micky. I wish they would get together. Do you remember back in England we were all so happy? Then Mum ran away with Ben, our teacher. I still love Mum, Don."

"Wish she hadn't gone away and left us, but now, we have a chance of being a family again. Sutra is just like granny, isn't she? She's warm and she smells of spice."

All this was said quite hushed to each other; neither of the boys wanted either their dad or Sutra to hear.

The brothers had stopped playing chess. The boys, Dennis and Sutra looked out at the sea, all very quiet and thinking of their own individual problems.

Sutra and Dennis found Lady Perrin, Dolly and David on deck staring out to sea.

"Horrible weather, isn't it? Shall we all go inside? I'm getting a bit wet and Sutra and myself need to ask you some more questions."

So, Dennis ushered all three women, plus the young man inside near a room that was used as a picture gallery seating them all near facing the windows and watching the rain splatter the glass.

"You three found the body."

"My daughter, Dolly, went in first. Dolly darling, what do you think was the time? Tell her."

"Do call me Dennis."

"Dennis, David, what was the time, dear?"

"Yes, Mrs err Gwen. I mean."

As David looked very hard at Gwen and smiled, she also smiled at him.

"Darling boy, what do you think?"

"About just before 11 A.M."

As he put his arm around Dolly's shoulder, she started to detail what she had seen.

"And I saw her near her cabin, talking to that nice American lady. That's when I said to her that I thought she looked quite sick and she was going to her cabin to lay down for a bit. Then I went to find Mum and David. We went down to the cabin; then, as my mum said, I went in first."

"What time do you think it was when you saw her and the American lady?"

"I think say 10 A.M.-ish; then I went back upstairs and found Mum and David near the restaurant."

"Thank you so much."

As Sutra wrote all this down on her pad, both she and Dennis turned back heading for the bar.

"Dennis, did you see what I saw?"

"What Sutra?"

"Lady Perrin had a small plaster on her neck and oozing from underneath it was a trickle of blood."

"Oh."

"Yes, could it be her? I'm wondering Let's find the American couple, they are sure to be in the bar."

It was about midday now, and the rain had really set in; very short howls of wind hit the windows. Sutra and Dennis found Stella and her brother in the bar, drinking a beer each with an ash tray full of cigarette butts, some smouldering while making a bluish haze above their table.

"Hi, there, another murder. That poor school ma'am! So, what are you two guys doing about this one?"

Sutra took this comment from Stella as being a bit sarcastic because she said it all with a slight smile on her face, but she let it go.

"Yes, it's all very unpleasant. We spoke to Dolly, the pretty English girl. She saw you with the dead women."

"Look here, honey; before you ask me the time, we all three were talking. I would say it was 10-ish she went upstairs and I wasn't going to leave that poor lady on her own, so we finished going down the staircase. We really should have taken the lift because she wasn't all that well, poor thing. Anyway, I put her to bed, gave her a couple of aspirins, made sure she was comfortable in bed and then left. Could only have been five or ten minutes more. I got into the lift and he was in it, that effeminate twit I took the lift with, up to the top floor; I got out and he said nothing; what could he say to me? Anyway, I would not bother saying anything to him. I'd rather smack him round the face; that sort makes me sick. They are not normal. I met my brother on the deck and we stayed there."

"Anyone see you up on the deck?"

"No, but if you have a word with that thing, I'm sure he'd say we were in the lift together."

"Thank you so very much. I'm sure you've been very helpful."

"Also, before I forget, a couple of days ago, the waiter was serving up tea, coffee and beef tea in the lounge; that was the day Mrs Handeisides was murdered. You may have been the last person to see her alive."

"Well, do you know after the waiter had given me a coffee, I turned around, saw her drop her knitting and I picked it up to let her to pick up her cup which she had put on a side board near the sliding door out to the deck. She then went outside, I think; I carried on to my brother; he was in the library, I think and that was the last I saw her. Oh, God, yes; I must have been the last to see her alive. Ooh, that sends a chill up my spine, honey; horrible!"

"Thank you so much."

"Sutra, I think we had better see Parul and sit down to discuss this all with her."

Dennis and Sutra whilst walking just outside the library bumped in to Mr Handeiside's.

Dennis questioned the American first. "We've just been talking to Stella."

"That bitch. Met her in the lift yesterday; she's a cow, can't stand her. I don't know why her brother doesn't get a life. He's always with her and she treats him like shit."

"Any idea what time that was and where did she go and where did you go?"

"Well, it would have been 11:10 A.M.; we went right to the top deck. She went towards one side; I went to the other to get as far away from that bitch as I could."

Chapter 8

Parul sat on her bed in her cabin reading her medical books, looking at different medications but coming up blank. She turned the page and came across a poison. Not quite what she was exactly looking for. She put a marker in the book and went looking for Dennis and Sutra. Both were still in the lounge staring out at the sea when Parul found them.

"I think I've found what I'm looking for. It's a poison called curare; it's from the Caribbean. It's made of a vegetable poison which acts by blocking the action of the neurotransmitter acetylcholine at neuromuscular junctions."

She waited so that Dennis and Sutra could take that statement in and then she carried on.

"Curare is used by the South American Indians and was formerly used as a muscle relaxant in surgery."

She once again took a breath before carrying on.

"My biggest problem is, that, it needs to be processed to a liquid before it can be used. This means that the first murder couldn't be just an off the cuff event. It had to be premeditated before the murderers came on to this ship; maybe weeks or months ago."

She took a deep breath.

"But, the second murder was, I'm, sure, done because Amelia saw the murder or murderers, as they were running away. Didn't she almost say that someone hooded ran into her and the hood fell off."

Pausing for a short while and then pointing her finger in the air, she continued, "Well, at that moment, if she didn't actually see the murderer, she must have worked it out. Then the murderer had to dispose of her."

She placed her hands on her hips.

"Oh my, what a terrible business this is," Sutra exclaimed. "I can see now, I'm sure!"

Sutra looked at Dennis before she carried on, "Dennis, what do you think of the situation? Parul has just about hit it on the nail, but, I would like her to explain this neuropterans?"

This time, Sutra faced Parul when she made this next statement. "My dear, you do need to explain in a way that I can understand."

Dennis shrugged his shoulder as he said, "So, what do we do now, Parul? We still have all these prospective murderers which we've all interviewed; nothing sticks out at all. The one and only person that could have known about the poison was the doctor."

"That's right, Dennis; but you know, when we interviewed him or we tried to, he was in the bar and he was so drunk, that, he fell off his stool and that waiter picked him up and took him down to his cabin. This poison, when ingested, will make the murdered victim alert yet unable to do anything like move or shout or prevent herself from harm."

Sutra told Parul about her questions to the American lady and of the plaster on Lady Perrin's neck and the blood too.

"We should question Lady Perrin about her injury. Why don't you question her, Parul; see what you think?"

"Yes, Dennis. I've got a lot to do?"

Parul set off to talk with Lady Perrin. Trying very hard to think how she was going to question her without her getting any idea that she thought she could be a suspect. All this going around in her head. She eventually found herself on the upper deck, it was now midday and two days before they got to the Australian coast.

The weather was hot and sunny but windy. The wind itself was very warm. She looked at the flying fish darting this way and that, cresting over the tops of the waves and spreading out their gossamer wings. Actually, flying on top of the crests of the waves just as if they were birds. She saw a seagull in the air, but then realised it was much bigger, A sea wanderer, an Albatross. Then she remembered from her school days about the wandering Albatross that could go flying far out from land. *We must be getting closer to land*, she thought.

Just standing there letting the wind blow her hair. How far she had come. Far from her homeland, India; even further from England and now, here she was on board a large ship steaming towards her future, with her aunty, Dennis and his two boys. She had a strange feeling for this man; not quite knowing what she felt, but, she knew her future was entwined with him.

Somehow, a future she was afraid of but also excited about. Even these murders, as horrible as they were, felt they were all part of a plan enmeshing her and them towards the future. She thought of Dennis, his face and his hair. He was not dark, yet his hair was black. His twin sons had blonde hair, not really looking at all that Indian. She smiled when she thought of him. She held her arms crossed around her waist, holding herself. She felt taller and she also felt very happy. She loved him being near; his smell and his touch. Her heart jumping when he came in to sight. Then, she snapped out of her revelry, as Lady Perrin, arm in arm with Dolly on one side of her and David on the other came walking towards her.

"Hello, getting closer to Australia, I think."

"Yes, Miss Das, not long now. How are you three getting on with the murders? Any nearer to finding out who did the killing?"

Parul wasn't sure how she should address Lady Perrin. Should she say Lady Perrin or what?

Lady Perrin realising Parul's problem, "Look, please call me Gwen."

Parul felt Gwen seemed different, more at ease. She certainly liked David far more than she did.

She also saw on her neck a small red blotch. Was it a pimple that had been burst or was it a scratch as Sutra was thinking. Lady Perrin realised that Parul was looking at her neck? She brought her hand up to pull the neck of her blouse up so that it covered it up.

"Would you mind if you all reviewed again what happened that night."

"Yes."

So, all three started to go through what they all previously said. Parul nodded from time to time until the full story had been retold.

"Are you very sure that you cannot remember anything else, however small you may think it is, or odd?"

"I'm sure that's all we can remember."

As Gwen nodded to both Dolly and David, they shook their heads.

"You all have been very helpful. Thank you so very much."

"It's such a nasty affair, isn't it? Who would have thought such a nice lady would be murdered on board a ship and why? I suppose you must think that anyone could have done the murder."

As she said this, she once again brought her hand up to make sure the scratch was hidden from Parul.

"Are there? Never mind, some people do some very nasty things, don't they, my dear."

"Oh, yes, they do, Lady; oh I mean Gwen."

Parul wanted so much to ask Lady Perrin why she was trying so hard to cover up the scratch, but if she did that, she would let the cat out of the bag; so she said her farewells and walked away still very uneasy. She couldn't get back to Dennis and Sutra quick enough to tell them of the meeting.

Parul pondered about Lady Perrin if she were the murderess. There could be another explanation to this conundrum. Once again, her feet took her to the deck; she stood leaning on the pivots of the life boat. I wonder if this life boat was ever launched. Looking along the deck between the metal strands that held the life boats in place, she then saw Benny Handeisides standing very close to where his wife had been murdered just staring at the spot. Suddenly, looking up as Stella walked through the sliding door from inside the ship.

"Good morning."

At that very moment, Parul dropped her purse that she was carrying. It fell into view with a large clatter. Benny looked around to where Parul was and quickly looked back at Stella.

"Why don't you leave me alone?"

Stella looked quite hurt by this remark then very quickly replied with a sarcastic remark, "I'm only trying to be civil; if you don't like me trying to be pleasant then go to hell."

Parul realised Benny had caught sight of her as she bent down to retrieve her purse. "Please don't mind me, I was looking out at sea."

"You're going, aren't you? Just go. Don't come near me."

Parul realised there was going to be another shouting match between them; so, she very quickly walked over so that she was now between them and both seemed to have calmed down. Stella turned around and walked away not before she turned her head around, stopped and just glared at Benny.

"I'm so pleased you turned up. We were going to have another screaming match. I really don't like that woman one tiny bit. She's a bully; a big fowl mouthed bitch! I feel so sorry for Simon; he's nice. When this is all over, I want to get to know him better."

"Bye."

Then turned, but didn't walk away just stood there. He didn't even wait for a reply, but Parul noted that he looked so sad with his head bent down, kicking an empty packet of cigarettes; then giving it one almighty kick, it spun in the air before it floated into the sea swallowed up by the waves.

"Bitch!"

He left Parul in a quandary. It didn't seem that he wanted his wife dead because being married to her, he would be able to carry on with his own sexuality and she didn't think his wife would have minded. She just needed a good-looking man around and she could do her own thing, and apart from that, he truly looked upset and was genuinely shocked by what had happened; and once Stella had found him with her brother, she hated him. There again, she had Lady Perrin with a scratch on her neck; if she killed the school mistress, she would have needed help. Could Dolly have been that person? And what about David also? She was sure that all three of them couldn't have murdered Mrs Handeisides; they didn't have time and anyway, Dennis, Sutra and herself agreed both murders were linked; so, whoever did one did the other.

Why? she thought. She had thought through all possibilities and nothing matched; but at times it did; who that was went around and around in her mind; she walked around the deck. Shall I get a cup of tea? No, then what? And where were Dennis and Sutra? Maybe they've come up with something; the more she rattled it around her head, the more everything got mixed up; it was driving her mad. She knew she had to solve this; she just had to.

She carried on walking around the deck and looking at the sea, until she saw the back of Sutra going inside through the sliding doors.

"Sutra, oh, Sutra," Parul waved as she shouted to her Aunty Sutra who turned and waved back.

"How far did you get with you know who?"

"I couldn't really ask her about the scratch but she did see me looking at it and covered it up."

She went over what she had been thinking about and both women more or less had come to the same conclusion.

"Where's Dennis?"

"He went to find the boys. We haven't seen them for some time. Boys, when they are left on their own, can get up to mischief. Well, those two certainly can and besides, we had been talking and trying to sort out things; and true, we came to a brick wall, Parul. We are all missing something. It's right there in front of our noses; once we find that small clue, it'll all knit together, I'm sure."

"I hope you are right. Why don't we find the men and play cards?"

Both ladies, linked arm in arm set off to find Dennis and the beasts.

After the ladies found Dennis and the twins, they all played a card game they had never heard of. Jonny had taught the boys one afternoon, and this game was called Eucha. The two boys were having such a lot of fun teaching the three adults this new card game. It was an odd night getting ready for dinner; eating the meal had no satisfaction. All three didn't have a great deal to talk about, plus, being on board for this length of time, they had these murders to solve; the trip was running thin. And they were getting bored; even the children had played the games they wanted to play and were getting fed up too.

After dinner, the boys went to the library to play chess. Parul, Dennis, and Sutra went on to the deck. It was still slightly light as they had decided to have an early dinner. It was warm, the sea was calm and not a ripple in sight. In the distance were dark billowing clouds. Lightning tore across the sky and the thunder rumbled in the distance.

"I think we are in for a storm."

Parul and Dennis cuddled up to each other. "Sutra, shall we call it a night?"

"There's a cold wind that just came up from nowhere; shall we stay here for a bit, Parul?"

"Just for a while; goodnight, Sutra."

"Yes, goodnight, you two."

Sutra went inside to get ready for bed in her and Parul's cabin and left Dennis and Parul together standing by the railing looking out at the storm slowly covering the sky with its tendrils of dark black clouds and its loud thunder and bright fork lightning.

"Come on, my dear, you really do look worn out. In fact, we all are. Let's have an early night. Anyway, it looks like we are going to get a storm."

So, they wandered hand in hand down to their cabins. Dennis deposited Parul outside her cabin and by now the ship was rolling quite a bit.

Parul kissed Dennis on the cheek. "Good night, my dear man."

"You too; sleep tight, my dear."

Then the fun started. The boat lurched, rolled and jumped every so often. A large bang would sound as if the ship had hit a rock and then lurched again and again. The heavens opened; lashings of rain hit in to the proud ship.

The boys were crying. Dennis had been thrown out of his bunk. He was holding tight to his crying sons.

In Sutra and her niece's cabin, it was even worse. Both ladies had sea sickness. Sutra was holding her stomach. With every lurch of the boat, both ladies heaved.

"Sutra, this is terrible. How are you felling now?"

The boat hit something with such a loud booming sound.

"Oh, this is horrible, what a joke."

"This is no joke. I'm sure we hit something! Oh, I don't care, oh god, ooh."

Both ladies were sick again, almost in unison this time.

Everyone on board was suffering. She lurched. She screwed through the great waves that hit her, cresting over her decks, chairs anything that wasn't screwed to the deck was washed overboard from side to side up down in to a deep trough then up high balanced on top of a large wave down again almost seemed as if the mighty ship was hitting the floor of the sea bed; all the passengers were either ill or afraid of the dark. The noise and the massive waves about, there were some that were afraid of being found out. The deep hate, lies and trying to cover up their involvement in the beastly murders; the heavens made them feel how monstrous they were, for committing such hellish crimes.

Dawn found the passengers either ill, bruised or battered. There were others with sprains even broken limbs. Breakfast found the three. They sat at their table, Sutra looked quite pale and had a black eye; she had fallen as one of the big lurches the great ship made shot her and Parul across the cabin, just missing a cabinet door that had opened and shattered as she hit it. Dennis and the boys faired a bit better; he had clung to them in a corner of their cabin while the boys cried. He had left the boys in bed to carry on sleeping while he came up to the breakfast room.

"Your eye, Sutra, are you all right? And what about you, Parul?"

"Oh, we are fine! That's the most dreadful night I've ever had and what's more, don't ever ask me to go on a ship again. How are you and the boys, OK?"

"Yes, we are all fine; just sat in the corner of the cabin with the boys. I've left them in bed. They had a harrowing night, poor kids."

The waiter came to their table and nodded, "The usual?"

"Jonny, these two I think, would like some coffee too."

The children that were present in the breakfast room were very subdued and their parents were not much better. Plenty of coffee was drunk. Earlier, Sutra had bumped in to the captain and he informed her that they had gone through a cyclone last night. He also wanted to enquire as to how they were all getting on with the murder investigations. She had informed him that they were making headway and would solve the murders well before they came to land; she assured him that once they were in possession of all the facts, they would hand the whole affair over to the Australian Police.

It was sunny now; the dark clouds had gone. The sky was blue again, chards of sunlight dappled in to the breakfast room making patterns on the ceiling.

"Milk. Cream."

All three were sitting clutching their empty cups.

"Would you mind bringing both? Why don't you two try milk; maybe cream?"

"To tell you the truth, my head is splitting, Aunty."

"Mine isn't much better, Sutra."

Once Jonny had brought the coffees, milk and cream, all three set to sort their individual likes and dislikes regarding coffees.

"Oh, boy. It certainly works, I mean I'm not great, but I think my brain is coming back to me at last. Shall we have a bit of a chat to sort a few things out?"

"I do feel we are getting somewhere but there's one very important piece of evidence we are missing. When we find it, I'm sure everything will drop in to place and I realise we've all gone through it before."

"Yes, Dennis, the whole thing keeps going around in my head; how many more days do we have before we reach land?"

"I think it's only one day now."

"Oh, surely not, Dennis."

"Yes, one that's all. Maybe it'll take a half day to get into port to dock."

At this remark from Dennis, Sutra folded her fingers together and looked at them.

"Don't worry, Sutra, we will all triumph, I'm sure."

They drank their coffee. Jonny their waiter topped their coffee's up. They eat ate toast, grapefruit marmalade and Feijoa jam. The boys turned up looking a bit blurry-eyed and yawning; yet, both, ate like lions, scoffing down whatever they could.

"What are you two going to get up to today?"

"Don't know, Dad. I think Don and I will go for a walk try to keep away from the girls. Tilly and that little girl, Badger, are great fun to play with; however, Bella's a right old misery gut. She was very horrid to Badger yesterday. She made her cry; we must keep away from her."

"Don't get in to trouble now."

"We won't, Parul; we are good boys."

"Yes. I'll believe that when I see it."

Both boys looked at all three adults, then turned and ran off giggling to themselves.

"I wonder what mischief they're going to get up to."

All three set off to find some dry deck chairs and just talk.

Chapter 9

Don and Michael thought it was such a nice day; they wolfed their breakfast down and left the three adults to their breakfast.

"Donny Boy, why don't we go and play shuffle board?"

Hoping that Don would agree, he thought may be Bella, who was still eating her breakfast with her parents, would not follow them as he didn't like her one little bit; she was a nasty little girl. She teased Don and he didn't like that. There was something quite horrid about her and he couldn't put his finger on it.

"I'd like that, Micky."

Off they went, passing by the swimming pool. They stood watching the other boys swimming; both felt a bit uneasy and neither wanted to get into the water. They had never been taught to swim, and so, it was fun watching the other boys playing in the pool.

"Hay, you two waner, come in," a boy with ginger hair called out.

"I'm Mark, come on; it's so warm."

Then all the other boys shouted.

"Come on, it's great."

Just as they were shouting, Don felt a large push from behind and he fell into the swimming pool, head first. He kind of twisted hitting his head on the side of the pool and sank to the bottom.

Looking up, he could see the legs of the other boys; a couple of men waved, their mouths opening and closing, and oh yes, Bella with her hideous smile. It sent shivers down him and then everything was calm; even his flaying about at the bottom of the pool. Blackness invaded his whole being.

"Grab him."

A man shouted as the pool started to change colour from blue to a crimson swirl; the other boys in the pool were franticly trying to get out. Some tried to dive down but none could find Don.

Another man pushed both Michael and the murderous Bella out of the way as he dived in to the pool locating the prone boy.

Dragging Don out of the pool like a wet fish, limp and lifeless, even Bella blanched as she realised what she had done and very quickly like the coward she was ran away crying.

Don opened his eyes; he could see the sky coughed and coughed. Michael was beside his brother, holding his hand and crying. The man that had pulled him out of the pool had given Don mouth to mouth. Everyone thought the boy was dead. Then he got up on one elbow, sinking back, coughing even harder and bringing up lots of water. Benny shouted out to anyone that could hear.

"Someone get the doctor. Are you OK, son? What's your name?"

"Don."

"Donny boy, oh, Donny," Michael stuttered out half shouting half crying.

"Oh, mate."

"He's going to be fine, young lad; don't worry." A man and a very young woman both put their arms around him.

"Ya OK, honey, yar gonna be fine."

Don recognised the nice American lady and the man was the husband of the American woman that he had seen a few nights ago dead.

"You're Benny."

"Just lay there until the doctor comes; there's a good boy."

Don could see the young woman looking so strange at Benny, but soon forgot as he saw the doctor was crouching over the top of him. Mr Bates, the ship's doctor enquired from the young boy what had happened.

"That horrible little girl Bella pushed my brother in to the swimming pool."

Stella looked at Benny.

"Oh, go on Benny, you tell him."

"That little girl, the shit, pushed him in and he hit his head."

The doctor took his pulse, looked at the big gash on the side of his head and mopped up most of the blood.

"Benny, pick him up and bring him down to the surgery."

"Martha, you bring his brother."

All four went down to the surgery.

"Lay him down."

Benny gently lowered Don to the table then the lady left. The doctor cleaned Don's gash on his head, stitched it, wrapped a bandage around his head and he fell asleep.

After sleeping for a long time, he woke up with a headache; his brother and Parul holding his hand. His dad and Sutra stood by. Sutra knelt down in front of Don. "How are you, my little pea?" Sutra stroked the hair out of his eyes.

"It was that horrid little girl, Bella; the one who's always smirking; I don't like that girl."

"Sutra, it was her. She pushed Donny in. I saw her when that man dived into the pool; she ran away crying, I hate her!"

"You must never say you hate anyone. That's not a nice thing to say, even if she's not a very nice little girl."

"But Sutra, I—"

"Listen to me, my other little pea; I love you both so much but you mustn't ever call any one that?"

Don thought about what Sutra had said. He then came up with what he thought would be a way of finding out what the word hate meant.

"Why, Sutra, hate is just a word; it means nothing."

"You are quite right. It is just a word like so many words in the English language; but, it's what it means; that's the problem. It's intense dislike for someone or malice towards a person."

Michael chirped up. "What does malice mean Sutra?"

"Oh, dear me; malice means that if you two boys don't stop asking me more questions I'll scream." Then she rethought her statement.

"I want you two to ask me anything at any time; that's the only way of learning and one day you'll have a wife each; she will be the one to teach you much more than I can."

"Why on earth would we want one of them? Just think; Micky, what would you do with them? You couldn't play games all day; what on earth would you do?"

"I da now, Donny."

Both shrugged their shoulders and both exclaimed, "Well, yes, we promise."

"That very nice American man dived in to save me and that nice American lady, Martha, helped him; they were so nice. I think they like each other."

All three adults were suddenly quiet. Parul asked Don, "Don, you say Martha was the name of that lady?"

"Yes, that's right."

Another long silence; the three adults looked from one to another. Parul addressed Dennis and her aunt, "It all fits now, doesn't it?"

Sutra and Dennis nodded.

"That's a bomb shell, Parul! It all fits now; that's the key we were waiting for, right, Sutra?"

Sutra agreed with Dennis.

"It all makes sense now, doesn't it? We had better get the captain to round up every one, Sutra."

Later that day, both boys were walking around the deck, when they bumped into Bella eating an ice cream.

All three stopped and stared at each other. Then, Don very quickly pushed the ice cream in to Bella's face.

"And that's from me."

Tilly, who had just come around the corner, stepped in between the boys and Bella. Tilly exclaimed, "You two, that's not the way to treat a little girl?"

With that comment, Bella beamed from ear to ear, but quick as a flash, Tilly pointed her finger at Bella lifting her chin up and onto her tip toes to her fullest height as she was just slightly shorter than Bella giving her the grimmest look.

"You are a very nasty girl and don't think for one minute I'm scared of you! These two might be, but not me! You're a nasty little bully and you pushed my best friend into the swimming pool. Didn't you realise he could have drowned? Then you would be a murderer and all murderers are horrible people. They go to prison. That's what my dad says. Go away, leave these two alone, now."

This last word, she shouted to Bella as loud as she possibly could, standing her ground against a much bigger girl and pushing her away from the two boys.

Both boys bursting in to fits of laughter as Bella just stood there dripping and fuming with anger; the ice cream was now down her dress, then giving out the loudest scream she ran away screaming and crying.

"Well, that's that, Donny."

"Micky, you're me man."

"I saved the day and I'm not afraid of her at all, Don. You're my best friend and besides, women have to stick up for their men."

As she said this, she bent and kissed Do; she then turned and danced away humming to herself, knowing she had won the day and she was going to make very sure she would keep her eye on her new found friend. This boy was hers from now on and apart from that, she felt very grown up and full of bristling electricity.

I'm a woman, not a little girl. The thought was well past her years but she felt fate changing what was to be.

The boys clapped their hands and danced away. Don looked back to the receding. Tilly had brought his hand to his mouth and then went as red as a beetroot; but with a very smug smile on his face. *Yes, that was my first kiss and I liked it,* he thought to himself then ran after his brother.

The three detectives skipped lunch; they all sat in the library and discussed what had happened earlier that day. Don being pushed into the swimming pool by Bella. The time both boys spent with the doctor and the revelations about the

American couple, how they were going to deal with it and which one of them would take charge of the proceedings and how it would roll out.

"I think one of us needs to take charge and quite frankly, I think it should be you, Parul. You are very calm and good at speaking and I'm sure we would both agree. We've got a bit of trapping to do because the culprits will not admit to the crimes unless trapped or put in to a situation where they feel they've got to own up; you are calm, a bit calculating and I don't mean that as an insult, Parul. You are well-trained as a doctor to wheedle out information from people who still are hoping that they are going to get away with these two murders. So what do you say, Sutra, do you agree?"

Looking at Parul, she said, "Dennis is right; she's the best person."

All this time, Parul was half listening to both Dennis and Sutra; she nodded from time to another not uttering a single word and when both of them had finished, Parul paused for a while thinking of possibilities how and what to say before she spoke.

"OK, I'll do it. Now, first of all, we've got to talk to the captain to get him to round up all the suspects. I think here in the library might be too small. What say we have it in the foyer between the bar and the restaurant? We could set up in the middle. There is a microphone at the side of the doors out to the deck just in case I need a mic. What do you think?"

Before they could answer, Parul carried on.

"I also think those doors need to be open to let some fresh air in because we are so close to the Australian coast; it's getting pretty hot and stuffy plus the foyer is in a sort of oval shape; I can or we can stand in the middle, so that, while I'm trying to trap the murderers, you both can keep an eye on every one, is that settled?"

Both Dennis and Sutra agreed.

"Now, I think, Aunty, you should talk to the captain and tell him what we've agreed to."

Parul paused for a short while and then resumed, "If we leave it to close to the coast, we would have to involve the

Australian police and I'd like to tie this all up before we get too close. If we involve them, they would want to talk to the suspects and let's face it; we now know who committed the murders, don't we?"

Taking a small breath, she carried on.

"Shall we start tomorrow late morning, which gives us all enough time to go over every single bit of evidence because we are dealing with vipers and vile ones at that."

Having another thought, "Oh, Dennis, I've got a job for you too. I want you, when I'm starting to speak, to walk around making sure everyone stays in the meeting. I do feel that, they think they've got away with it and to suddenly be asked to attend this meeting, they might suspect something. Anyway, I want everything to go perfect."

Both agreed. Sutra went off to see the captain while Parul and Dennis sat quite in the library.

They all got dressed for dinner and after Sutra went to bed, Dennis and Parul walked around the deck of the boat; she put her hand in his and shivered slightly not because she felt cold, nor that it was cold the evening was warm and sultry. A slight tropical breeze rustled through her hair. The sky was a blaze with stars. They stopped at the very front of the ship both looking ahead. Her white silken scarf blew in the breeze; it fluttered in to Dennis's face catching on his shaven chin; wrapping it around his neck as if it were a snake and yet drawing them closer and closer yet almost touching. She looked into his eyes and saw her future. She saw for the first time, in her life, the one human in this whole world that she knew she wanted to be with for the rest of her life; she looked at his eye lids. She had never noticed that Dennis had such long eye lashes, almost feminine. She touched his face with her fingers so lightly as if by a feather.

He gazed at the woman he knew he loved. He too shivered. Her face, her strong almost chiselled jaw, yet, so beautiful like a flower that had just been dipped with dew at its first opening to the sun. Her hair tied back with that butterfly clip holding it back; he felt her wisp of fingers touching his face. Nothing in the world mattered.

Then, a sharp blowing from the ships whistle, as another ship passed by; tourists were hanging on the rails waving to the ship passing; the moment was broken and both lovers were awoken as if from a dream.

"It's getting cold, Dennis; shall we go inside?"

He nodded, half in his wondrous dream and half in reality. He walked Parul to her cabin and said good night.

She opened the door, hesitated and he put his hand over hers.

"Is that you, Parul?" Sutra called to her niece.

Sutra had nearly choked herself on a very large snore which brought every one back to reality.

All three went to bed thinking of what was going to happen tomorrow. They would unravel and expose the murderers and finally, the whole business would come to an end.

Parul, Sutra and Dennis all had the sleep of a lifetime. Both boys twisted in their sleep.

Don was dreaming of the kiss, Michael of Badger and Bella fighting a duel over him; both determined to win his favour.

Tilly dreamed walking with a handsome young man down the aisle, looking in to Don's face pledging her life to his. Badger dreamed of Michael and smiled.

Bella had a nightmare. Shouting out loud, "Michael, I'm so sorry; I'm sorry!" She then let out a cry and woke up crying.

Both parents woke up. Her mother got out of bed, knelt down putting her arm around her daughter and smoothing the hair from her. Her father, Ted, just lay on his side watching his wife, Eva console the child.

"What's up, darling? Had a bad dream?"

As Bella cried in her mother's arms, "I'm a very evil girl. I could have murdered Don and I've pushed Michael away, Mummy. I couldn't help myself, I'm so bad."

As she broke down crying even harder.

"There, there, my sweet. You're only a little girl and your dad and I care for you so much. I know you pushed that little boy in to the swimming pool and it wasn't a good thing to do. Now, it doesn't mean you're evil; don't let your emotions get the better of you. Now, you need to learn the fact, that, you admitted to yourself and us that you didn't like what you did; you've learnt something, haven't you?"

Ted got out of bed and knelt next to his wife holding his wife around the shoulders and his other hand stroking his daughter's head.

"Listen to your mum, sweet heart; you've suddenly grown up."

"Mum, Dad, I'll never be bad again!"

All three got back in to bed and slept; all the passengers slept. The moon shone down on the mighty ship as she drove through the waves. But four humans tossed and turned. One let out a cry of anguish like a tormented soul, the others twisted and turned. Another cried in hate. The two others woke.

Arthur got out of bed, went to the toilet, then sat on his bed, took the bottle of booze he had almost finished earlier and downed the last dregs. A lone figure walked the top deck; the wind dragged at his clothes. His hair ruffled; he pulled his dressing gown tighter around him. His body was cold as ice. Evil was in him but also love for the woman he loved so much and the one he had murdered for.

Rounding the deck, *what was it? Moonlight? Or was it her standing, staring at him and mocking him.* He looked down at his hands. They were covered in dripping blood; he screamed and covered his eyes, but, he knew she was still there. He had murdered his wife. He came to a stand-still looking down at the spot where he had murdered his wife; he cried. Tears trickled down his cheeks and dripped down on to the deck. Then, he woke up crying, sitting on the side of his bed swaying back and forth holding himself.

Chapter 10

They all got up early and had their breakfast. Dennis told the boys to go, find Tilly and Badger and play shuttle board. Sutra explained to Parul and Dennis what she had told the captain and the agreed time in the foyer. She had given a list of whom she wanted to be there and also, to be sure of the general set up of the chairs in the foyer. The captain had told the barman and Jonny the waiter to set up everything for 11 A.M.

Slowly, every one settled in to their chairs with Parul standing in the middle with Dennis and Sutra on each side.

David, Dolly and her mother looked sombre. Lady Perrin had a dark midnight blue dress on with the buttons of the dress buttoned tight across her neck with matching blue shoes, white leather gloves. She had a small blue hat on the side of her head with a small light blue feather in the brim. Dolly had a full yellow dress with a red poker dot scarf around her neck and yellow slip on shoes.

The American brother and sister sat next to them. Stella sat with her back to Parul. She wore a full red dress just over her knees with red, high-heeled shoes and chatted to Helen Mac Clures. Her husband, Cameron, was quiet. Fred Lear sat with his legs apart leaning back in his chair; it looked as if he were almost slipping off the chair. The captain and the doctor stood to the sides of the oval foyer; the doctor seemed much more sober. Benny Handeisides slouched up against the wall smoking a cigarette. Jonny and the bartender stood next to Benny.

"Thank you so much everyone to take the time to come to the foyer. As you know, the captain asked myself, my aunty and Dennis Galvin to look into these two murders. After we all interviewed you, we came to a number of conclusions. So,

I'd like to start by going over both crimes with you all; a sort of summary of each murder."

She paused here for a small breath then carried on.

"Mr and Mrs Handeisides were on a cruise eventually going to England and Europe. On their way to Australia, Mrs Handeisides was murdered at about 6:14 P.M. On the fourth day of the cruise, the ship's doctor, Mr Arthur Bates, stated, she was slain by three knitting needles; two went straight in to the chest and pierced the heart; the third went halfway into the chest. So, we've come to the conclusion, that, there were three murderers and one accomplice."

Clearing her throat, she carried on.

"The second murder was committed because poor Miss Amelia Stamp saw something and she had to be silenced; she was murdered at about 10 A.M. the next day. Stella Rudd was the last person to see her alive."

At that moment, Stella gave her brother a slight smile and hung her head down, looking very upset. She put her hand to her head and she started to weep. Simon, seeing this, put his arm around his sister's shoulders.

"It's all right, Stella; you're upset, aren't you? Are you sure you were the last to see the old dear before she was murdered?"

At this statement, Stella started sobbing. Fred Lear, got up and walked to the prone girl. "Don't upset your self-love!"

"If only I had stayed with her, she wouldn't have been murdered! Oh my God, I can never forgive myself, never." And rocked back and forth wailing far more than she had. Fred placed his hand on the young women's shoulder to console her.

Parul carried on with her scenario of the murders. "She put up quite a fight, didn't she, Lady Perrin?"

"Miss Das, when we three got there, we could see by the state the cabin was in, that poor lady must have struggled a lot. The bed was in a big mess."

Having said that, Lady Perrin brought a small brightly coloured handkerchief out of her handbag and brought it to her nose dabbing it. Now, Parul looked straight at Lady

Perrin; Parul looked at her hands out stretched on her lap; both hands were shaking. Parul carried on with her cross examination of Lady Perrin.

"She put up quite a fight for someone so small and slim. But this time, something happened that the murderer wasn't expecting. She put up such a great fight for her life and in doing so, she scratched her murderer because on the pillow was blood and also on the sheets so the murderer has a scratch somewhere?"

Lady Perrin brought her hand up to her neck where Sutra had first seen the plaster and the trickle of blood; she pulled the collar up of her dress, gave a slight gasp and started to cry.

This time Parul almost spat the words out, "Isn't that right, Lady Perrin?"

Parul raised her voice again as she did. There were gasps all around. Benny made a sudden rush for Lady Perrin; she put her hands up and tried to run but slipped. Dennis came between Benny and Lady Perrin, who was weeping and sat on the floor with David, protecting her as if he were a lion.

Dolly had her fingers raking through her hair and David shouted out, "Gwen would never do anything so terrible; she's a sweet lady?"

"You, old bitch; you murdered my wife. I loved her!"

More gasps from everyone, Helen burst in to tears; her husband, Cameron, holding his wife tightly. The barman and Jonny looked surprised.

"No. You didn't murder Mrs Handeisides," said Parul, "Even though you have a plaster on your neck, it's hiding a small pimple isn't it."

"Ya, ya, yes."

"You couldn't have, but someone did. As I said, both murders are linked. I'll go back to the first murder. How on earth did a woman knitting allow herself to be brutally murdered without a fight? The watch was broken; it was altered by the murderers so that would give them an alibi. The cup was smashed too."

She paused for a short moment to let this sink in.

Everyone in the foyer was quiet.

"The cup had to be smashed because that's where the poison was in, so the prone victim could see her murderers and not move; she could do nothing?"

More gasps. Benny looked at Stella in a very angry way. She tossed her head back and showed her pearly white teeth.

Parul knowingly addressed Mr Bates, "Isn't that right, Mr Arthur Bates?"

Arthur looked at Benny and shouted at him, "You shouldn't have killed the old girl?"

Before he could get the words out, Benny shouted at him, "Shut up you stupid drunk."

This time, Stella ran to Benny. He held his arms up to protect her. She sank her head in to his chest weeping. He put his hand on the back of her head stroking her hair and kissing her neck; they then kissed passionately.

"Darling, we knew this could happen! I would do anything for you; I love you so much!"

"And I love you, my sweet man."

Benny faced Stella, "You know what we have to do now?"

"My darling."

Clasping each other in a hug, then parting and in unison shouted out for the heavens to hear, "I love you."

The whole crowd was in an uproar. The captain tried in vain to calm things down. Then, before anyone could stop them, they ran through the sliding doors out to the deck mounted the railings and holding hands and staring just one last time at each other before they plunged in to the sea. Everyone ran to the railing. Dennis got there first. He made a grab for Benny's jacket but it tore off. They were over and gone before he could do a thing.

The sea was blue; not a ripple. They surfaced once more; the waves closed over their heads and they disappeared out of sight. Two dark fins circled where the lovers had entered the blue sea. They swam around for a short time; then, a slight crimson; soon darker crimson; the sea thrashed about with dark fins' and blood. Arthur Bates was weeping and, on his knees, blubbering out something that couldn't be understood. Simon had his hands to his face crying uncontrollably.

"Martha. Oh god, Martha. Martha. What am I going to do? Oh my God. Please, God forgive me!" he shouted as he sank to his knees, looking up to the sky with his hands clenched together as in prayer. Cameron had taken his coat off and thrown his shoes off in an effort to dive in to the sea but Helen and Sutra pulled him back. Parul just stood at the railings shaking, seeing this hell break out. Then, a shard of sun light shone on the passengers, bathing them in sunlight and peace as if the heavens approved of what had just transpired; all that could be heard were the gulls screeching; they now started to weal around the ship. Martha's brother, Simon, wept uncontrollable and Arthur Bate was in total shock.

Parul looked to the horizon and saw land just a speck. She started to cry, but quick as a flash, Dennis was at her side, holding her for all his might. Sutra was busying herself helping to calm Lady Perrin, who, by now had lost her hat in the sea; her hair was wet with her crying. Her daughter, Dolly, was holding her mother and David was holding both ladies.

"Don't cry; please don't. I'll take care of you. I'll never leave you; never ever!"

"Oh Davy?"

Even Jonny had a tear. The barman pretended not to, but blew his nose and wiped his eyes.

"This is a rum business, Jonny Boy." clapping the waiter on his back as he said this.

Parul took hold of Dennis's hand, "Now what, Dennis?"

"Parul, we just get on with our lives and look to the future. We all have a bright future in a new land that we will call our home?"

Both looked to the horizon to a new day a new dawning.

The captain had his staff help both Simon and Mr Bates to his cabin. The door was locked, and guarded just in case either thought they too could escape justice.

Parul faced the captain.

"Captain, could we interview Simon and Mr Bates; we know they were involved with the murder but I want to hear the story from the beginning."

"Yes! That's fine. I'll order my staff outside just in case you have any problems."

"Captain, the worst has gone; they should not be a problem at all."

When they all got inside, Sutra sat on a settee next to the captain's bed; Parul and Dennis were on the bed. The two prisoners were sitting in two armchairs. Parul looked at Steven.

"Well, do you want to start with the whole story, Simon?"

Simon hung his head low as he started his story.

He stuttered a bit before he started, "Well, err, we, erm."

He clicked his tongue as he cleared his throat then began again.

"I'm not sure where to begin."

"From the very beginning," Parul said. Parul sounded a bit abrupt mostly because she didn't have much sympathy for them. Her aunty was drumming her fingers on a nearby coffee table which seemed to add to the electrified air in the cabin.

Dennis just looked straight ahead at a painting of a boy catching a butterfly in a net seeming not at all interested in the whole preceding. Then, he suddenly launched out in a sudden flurry of words aimed at the very scared Simon, "Come on, tell us?"

Simon obeyed at last and started his story.

"My name is Steven and not Simon. Martha and I had a good father. He had made his fortune in stocks and shares. Our mother, his wife Ruth, was part Sioux Indian. He married her later in life. His marriage with our mother was a love match; she died in childbirth having me. My older sister, Martha, was six at that time and between her and my father, they brought me up. We were a happy family until she came."

He snarled, "She wanted our father and his money; not us; besides, we both were older. We were pushed aside. Both of us went to New York to work and took on new names. By that time, we knew she had much influence on our father. He turned against both of us and wrote us out of his will. She was determined to take full control of everything."

He looked up and then at the painting Dennis had been looking at then the ceiling. As if he suddenly had awoken from a dream, he stuttered and starting back to his story.

"We didn't hear much from our father until he got ill. His manager, Bill Danby, of the ranch phoned me and informed me he had passed away quite quickly. That bitch got everything. By then, I worked as a waiter in a restaurant in Brooklyn. My sister worked in a department store; we were happy but talked a lot about how Ethel had come between us and our father. It hurt Martha so much. She loved both our parents."

He spread one of his hands on his leg; rubbing up and down the leg, he cleared his throat and resumed his is story.

"One day, while she was eating her lunch in the park, a stranger got talking to her. This was Benny; eventually they fell in love. She told him our story. We three dreamed up a way of getting even with that bitch," He smiled to himself and then carried on again, "Benny agreed the best thing was to meet Ethel and get her to marry him. But, at first, we needed to get them to meet, and so, Benny moved to the town where she lived. They met at a ball and he cultivated his effeminate way, so, she would see him as a husband only in name; they married and then it was easy for him to get Ethel to go on a cruise after their wedding."

Pausing for some breath and straightening his back, he began again, "We booked on the same ship, but at that stage, we hadn't got a plan." He smiled a sad smile. "I didn't like the murder one bit; but what else could we do? We had to make her pay."

This time, he stopped for quite some time. Sutra faced him. "Well, what next? How did you expect to get away with this, young man?"

"Things suddenly dropped into place quite by accident. I got talking to Arthur Bates. He came in to the restaurant one rainy night and was very drunk to have a meal; and so, between myself and Sam, my friend, we took him back to our apartment as he was very drunk. We thought it would be better if he sobered up in our apartment before he went back to his hotel."

"I remember that night I got so drunk. I knew the ship was sailing in four weeks on a round the world cruise. Steven, you were kind to me. I was very low and unhappy; I told you my story!"

Sutra looked from him to Steven.

"Yes, Arthur, we got talking later after Sam left for work."

"That's right and I—"

Steven then interrupted Arthur, "You can tell them your story when I'm finished; so, shut up and wait till it's your turn."

"OK! OK! No need to get so upset, mate."

"Don't mate me, you drunken sod."

"That's enough, you two. There are ladies present. You should think about them and I advise you to get on." Dennis was now getting very cross.

"Arthur and myself got drinking. He told me his life story and we both realised he had known Ethel years ago. She had been his girl and it just so happened, that, he was the ship's doctor; on the ship that Benny and she were on. The next day, I introduced him to my sister and Benny and I came up with this plan."

Both nodded at each other.

"We were going to murder just her. Arthur had been so hurt by Ethel when she refused to marry him."

"Over the years, I came to hate her."

"You hated her that much?" Sutra said this half to herself and to Arthur.

"I thought of poison Curare was the best option."

"We told him what she had done to us. He agreed to get the Curare and bring it on board even if he were searched. Arthur felt he could talk his way out of anything. Anyway, anyone who suspected anything wouldn't worry about it because he is a doctor; so, everything was in place."

"I hated Ethel. I wanted her dead, but this whole thing went far too far out of hand."

After this outburst. Arthur sat still with his hands in his lap and may be this was the very first time he'd actually had been sober.

Steven resumed his tale of the murders.

"Martha started our plan by slipping the poison in to Ethel's cup as she put it down while adjusting her knitting. We waited till it took its effect. Then we three took her knitting needles. First, Martha drove her needle in as she shouted through her gritted teeth, remember me, you bitch? I'm Doug's daughter! Remember? I'm Martha."

Steven stopped for a small breath. Then resumed telling his story.

"I drove the needle in but I couldn't get it right through. I said, I'm Steven. Remember, this is for Dad and Ruth, our mum."

Then, Benny, Ethel's husband looked at Ethel. "Do you honestly think I loved you? You're a painted old crow that feeds on life. Now take this," he said, as he drove his needle as far as he could. "We then realised, that, she was dead. Benny took her watch off and changed the time, so that, we would have an alibi. I smashed the cup, we all split up and we were meeting in our cabin. Martha ran in to the school ma'am and while she ran, her hood came off slightly. She was sure the old dear had recognised her."

He waited a bit, sighed to himself, and then began again.

"Before the murder, we had set up our alibi. We set up the charade. Benny took most of his clothes off, just leaving his trousers on. I took my clothes, got on to the bed and Benny got on top of me."

"Good plan; what a sham. It could all have worked, if you hadn't killed the old dear."

"What you really mean is keeping your mouth shut."

"OK! OK!"

"We all started to shout and pretend to fight; we made sure we would be heard by someone in the corridor. The old school ma'am walked past our cabin, and that's when Martha ran out, screamed at Benny, after slapping him in the face. We made sure she saw us fighting when she had gone passed; we had to run up the stairs to commit the crime and as I said before, changing the time on her watch giving us the perfect alibi."

He stopped and cleared his throat, "We then had to kill the school ma'am. We thought she might realise we were the murderers. Martha had met the school teacher on the staircase and accompanied her to her cabin; she then left. We knew we had to do this quickly, so, we went back to her cabin. Benny grabbed the pillow, Martha held her down on the bed and I kept watch at the door. He bit his nail off; he had it in his teeth then spat it on to the floor. She put up one hell of a fight and scratched Benny's wrist. When we were sure she was dead, I ran up the stairs. I nearly ran in to that lady her daughter and boyfriend; Martha and Benny took the lift."

"Why the hell did you have to kill the old dear? Why, Steven, that should not have happened."

"What about you, doctor?"

"He has said mostly all I was going to say, but, there was no need to kill Miss Stamp; she was a nice lady. She didn't see Martha at all."

"She did." Steven shouted and lunged over to the doctor and grabbed him by the scruff of his neck and shook him like a bag of old cloths.

"If you hadn't opened your big mouth, we might have got away with it. All you needed to do is keep your cool; but oh no, you couldn't do that, could you? Now Martha and Benny are dead and we are left to carry the task out, you idiot!"

These last few words Steven had shouted to the doctor, prompted Dennis to come in between them and with Sutra's help, he calmed things down. Parul turned to the doctor and looked him straight in the face. He hung his head low and then put his face into his hands. Parul now addressed the doctor

"Well, Mr Bates?"

"Everything he said was correct. I was drunk at the restaurant and yes, I told Steven my story. Oh yes, I hated Ethel and I did get the Curare and yes, I distilled it. Had it in my medical case. I thought if any one questioned me about it, I'd say it was just a sleeping draft and that's that."

Steven interrupted, "We were able to use it."

"Hey, I was quiet while you went on and on. Shut up Steven! Let me talk."

"Shut up! Oh, you want to talk now, Arthur do you?"

Dennis had just about enough with these two bickering.

"I think that's enough. Now carry on," Dennis shouted and looked crosser than Parul had ever seen him.

"I felt nobody would question me about it; but after she was killed, I felt ashamed of myself. I couldn't get her face out of my dreams and my nightmares. I remembered when we were young, how stunning she was and how I loved her. How she dashed my dreams too. Oh God, please forgive me as I can never forgive myself. I don't care what the sentence is; I'll never ever be a real man and Miss Stamp, why? Why?" He started to weep.

"Oh, shut up! You knew what you were getting yourself into; don't try kidding yourself, buster!"

"So, now what, Miss Das?" Steven pouted. Steven spread his hands on his lap almost as if both hands were fans.

"Mr Leadbetter and Mr Bates, you will be kept here guarded until we reach Freemantle. Once there, we will hand you over to the Australian police. They will be waiting for you. Our job is over now. We will not be meeting again!"

At that, all three detectives rose and vacated the cabin, went up to the fresh air of a brilliant late afternoon to enjoy what time they had on the ship.

"Well, my dear, you've cracked it. Parul."

"Dennis, it doesn't make me feel good, but, we all have triumphed haven't we?"

"Parul, I'm an old lady and I've seen things. I saw your father and mother after the crash. I had to identify them and from that moment on, you were my child; the one I never had. But, darling girl, I knew there was something that fate had in store for you and I'm so very proud of you."

With that, Sutra gave a few sniffs and a tear ran down her face while gathering both her loved ones in her arms. All three stood there watching the Australian coast and the seagulls sweeping overhead.

The ordeal was over, justice had been done, but had it? Was there another murderer on-board the ship? Was everything cleared up and will this murderer see justice? All three detectives thought it was over, but, there still lurked a murderer amongst them. Unknown and not forgiven, a crime so foul.

Chapter 11

Overnight, the Electra steamed into Fremantle. A tug had pulled the massive ship to the docks, where in the early morning gangs of workers had fastened her to the dock and the whole wharf was full of bustle. The boys were up with quite a few children, Tilly and Badger stood near the boys; Bella stood on her own. She was looking at Michael. She twisted a few strands of hair in her fingers, as she looked at him. Then, her parents took her downstairs to go for a day trip to Perth. All the children chattered and laughed excitedly. Adults were looking at their new land. Fred felt empty. He would make a new life for himself on the Gold Coast but he knew he would never find a woman like Ethel; never.

The Australian police were now on-board and in the lounge. All three detectives were informing the police what had happened on board the vessel. They had already taken Arthur and Steven. Both left the ship with heads hung low. Then put in to a waiting black car that sped to a waiting jail.

"Come on, Cameron. Let's go up to see the New World. Don't forget, we've still got a fair way to go before we get to Sydney?"

"Yes, mi dear! Have I ever told you, you're the one and only one for me?"

Cameron kissed his wife tenderly on the cheek, "Oh, don't get soft on me, ya great lump."

Tilly's mother and father had stayed on-board and had become very friendly with Badgers parents; Mark and Eva Spencer and were seated at the bar. They realised they were going to New Zealand.

"My uncle Dick passed away a few months ago and left me his property on the Canterbury plains near a town called

Fairlie. It's got flocks of sheep on it and what they call a share milkier farming it. Eva and I thought we would come out to take a look at it to see what's to learn and maybe try farming ourselves."

"Yes, dear." Eva's eyebrow raised as she said this with a bit of laughter, "He thinks. Well, my farm boy, we shall see."

"We are staying with Jenny's Aunty Claire at her large house on the beach at St Helier's Bay, Auckland. It sounds really nice, where we will eventually settle. I'm not sure but we will take a trip around New Zealand and see. It would be nice to call in and see you both and your farm."

"Yes? Why not."

The men carried on chatting while the ladies talked over the past events on board the ship. Leaving the two girls to once again to capture their two victims. All four children were sat in a circle on the top deck.

"What are you going to do when you grow up Tilly?"

"I'm going to marry you." She was looking at Don in a rather sheepish way.

"What? Ha. Ha. Me?"

"Yes, of course."

As if Don should know.

"I would like to know what you two boys are going to do," Badger said this statement rather matter of fact.

"Well, Micky and I are going to open a restaurant in Auckland. We are going to be the most famous chefs in New Zealand."

Then, all three children started chattering about what they were going to do when they grew up leaving Badger chewing her long red hair with a secret wish of her own; she could see herself on his arm in front of the vicar, saying "Yes, I do," as she gazed in to the eyes of the boy she loved.

By this time, Parul, Sutra and Dennis were now on deck standing and looking at all the commotion going on as passengers walked down the gang plank to customs and their new country.

Parul wore a slim pencil dress; it was white with delicate red flowers. She wore a white hat with a dainty red feather which trailed down just sitting on the side of her head. They were standing chatting, when, from the gang of men working on the docks, a shrill shout went out from one very burly Aussi workman.

"Hay, mate. Are ya gonna kiss her?"

"Me?"

"Yes, you! Why don't you kiss that Sheila while you're still young?"

Dennis took her in his arms and kissed her. She felt giddy. She couldn't hear the shouts from the workers as they threw their hats in the air and shouted with all their might. She didn't hear the wolf whistles and the noise of the cranes as they lifted the baggage from the holds of the ship. Neither did she hear the gulls up on high screeching as small morsels of food were dropped into the sea from the kitchens.

She heard nothing; the world had stopped and for the first time in her life, she knew what she wanted and that was his arms about her his soft tender lips on hers; her heart pounding to the rhythm of her blood pumping around her body; this was it. Her hat blew off in to the sea. It fluttered gently down to the waiting waves. She hadn't a care about it; he was all she wanted.

Dennis could feel her heart beating like a small bird that he had just captured. Fluttering, trying in vain then giving in to pure love. He held her in his arms. He knew he had found the one and only woman in the world that made life worth living.

The boys were being hugged by Sutra. "Boys, never forget, that, love always triumphs for every bit of hate; there is love. And those two are in love. We are now one family. I love you both, I'm such a lucky lady."

The commotion from the workers still carried on that included whistles and shouts. One burly workman grabbed his tall and thin mate; they did a jig. By now, the passengers on board saw the lovers enmeshed in each other's arms. Helen jabbed Cameron in the ribs.

"Well." Cameron exclaimed.

"Well what?"

"Oh? You come here, you lump."
"Oh this."
"Yes? My great big bear."

As she kissed him, she parted just looking at this man of hers.

"Come here, my woman; you're not getting away with just one kiss."

Then he held her in his arms as they hugged and kissed.

By now, the people on the wharf and the ship were in an uproar. Such happiness, that, Sutra joined in with the uproar, clapping her hands until she couldn't clap any more.

The children were on the deck. Tilly looked at Don, smiled and then blew a kiss. Don caught it. Badger twisted her red hair around her finger while Michael looked at her.

Lady Perrin, Dolly and David slowly walked the deck taking in the air and the bright sun. She had her dark red umbrella up shading her pale skin; Dolly's hair was caught in the wind strands of it blew over her eyes. David caught one strand, held it in his fingers and felt the lustre of the hair and smelt the perfume she wore. Caught in the revelry of love, he looked at her; this young woman he had so passionately fallen in love with. The way she held herself, it was almost like a leopard. She languidly fluttered her eyelashes at him and gave him the most brilliant smile.

"Penny, your thoughts, my dear?"

"I wasn't thinking of a thing; just looking at my lady-love."

But David thought how far he had come and what he had done. He looked at Dolly with much love and Gwen he had grown to like her. Maybe she was the mother he always wanted; she wasn't a bad old tart after all. He then cast his mind back many years. His father had run away with David's school mistress, Gail. It broke his mother's heart; she turned from a loving mother to a monster, never letting her son out of her sight. So, whenever a girl got close to him, she frightened her away. He felt bullied by his mother and over the years and he came to hate her. He planned to some day run away too like his father, but, she would find him, he knew.

Eventually, he came up with a plan; one day making sure Edwina was soundly a sleep from the sleeping draft he had given her. He dragged her sleeping body to the gas stove. Placing a pillow on the oven door and then placing his mother's head on the pillow, he stroked her hair, lovingly kissed her forehead and then turned the gas on full. Going out of their house by the back door and closing it so softly, nobody would ever know he murdered his own mother.

Only you.

THE END